# PART ONE:
# NEW BOY

# roll
# dem
# bones

# roll
# dem
# bones

*Nicholas Bruner*

Roll dem Bones
© 2020 Nicholas Bruner

ISBN  978-1-7354892-0-9

# CHAPTER ONE

He stood near the high school cafeteria door with a tray in both hands, scanning the room for a friendly face. His nose wrinkled in response to the greasy sour stench, the kind of smell that slithers in your nostrils and rolls down your throat. The smell of this cafeteria was worse than most, and he'd been in plenty.

The place was packed with kids sitting at tables, waiting in line for food, or crowded around the exits in chatting, laughing, gossiping knots. It was embarrassing standing there holding his tray, and he knew from experience the longer he went without making a move, the worse it would get. The only consolation was that everybody else seemed too wrapped up in themselves to notice him much.

He spotted a round table over in a corner with several empty chairs. A lone girl sat there, dark-skinned, her hair neatly braided and tipped with bright blue beads. Promising. The boy edged his way through the cafeteria, holding his tray high on his chest to avoid bumping anybody.

*Should I ask if the seats are free?* he wondered. *No, too risky. Don't give her a chance to think about it.* He decided a better strategy would be just to sit like it was no big deal. He lowered his tray to the table.

The girl put her sandwich down and said in a loud voice, "Excuse me, that seat is taken."

"I'm s-s-sorry," the boy said. "It d-didn't look like anyone was here."

"Well, that's your mistake now, isn't it?" the girl replied. He wished she would turn down the volume a little bit. He sensed kids at nearby tables turning to stare. Better to cut this off now, before his face flushed and his throat tightened even more. He picked up his tray and slowly turned back around, desperate now for a place to sit. It was even worse than before—not only was the cafeteria still jammed, but now he saw a few kids recognizing his predicament, their lips curling in anticipation of preying on weakness. No matter. He'd lived through worse. He took a deep breath and shifted his weight to take a step.

"Hey, boy, wait a minute," the girl called to him. Something struck her about this slight, pale kid with little wisps of red hair swirling uncombed on his head. Some bit of steel in his backbone, some hint he wasn't as pitiful as he looked on the surface. "You might as well sit here a minute. You know, 'til all my friends get here."

Not a great bargain but he took it. "Th-th-thank you," he said, putting his tray back down. He wanted to explain about how hard it was to find a friend, or at least a seat, but it was better to keep the words inside. Inside they were clear and strong, outside they were muddled and brittle.

"So you got a stutter, huh?" she said.

"Yes," he said. "I c-can't help it."

"I know that. Nobody would stutter if they could help it, would they?"

The boy shook his head.

"My name is Dice. I mean, it's not my real name. But it's what ever'body calls me." The boy smiled and moments passed. Dice tapped impatiently on the table a couple times. "Now, you tell me your name," she said with a roll of her eyes, irritated at having to explain the basics.

"I'm S-Sullahan," he said.

"Sullahan? What kind of name is that?"

"It's f-from Ireland."

"I don't mean, where is the name from," she said. "I mean, why is it so weird?"

He shrugged and brought a bite of lima beans to his mouth. "Y-you're one to talk, D-dice."

Dice made a clicking sound in the back of her throat like he was pushing his luck. "All right. I'll call you Sully for short. How do you like that?"

"It's fine," Sully said. "Other k-kids have worse n-n-n-_"

"Worse names for you," Dice said. "Got it. So, you new here, huh?"

"Yes, I j-just moved here."

"Where'd you come here from?"

"From T-t-tenne-tenne-"

"Okay, Tennessee. Look, I'll do the talkin', and you just eat your lunch, okay?"

Sully nodded. Not talking was fine with him.

"What's that?" she asked, pointing to a tiny silver pin on the collar of his shirt. It was in the shape of triple spirals meeting in the center.

He tapped it without looking. "A g-good luck charm. M-my mom gave it to me. It's called a trisk-k, a triskel-l—"

"Don't bother. Does it work?"

"N-not really."

Dice lost interest in the triskelion. Her eyes brightened with a new idea. "Rules."

"R-rules?"

"Yep. If you're going to be sittin' here every day, there's going to have to be some rules. Number one, this is my table, and I can tell you to go any time." She checked to see if he was paying attention. Sully chewed a bite of Salisbury steak and gazed at her. Good enough. "Two, I make all the rules. As long as you're sittin' here, I can tell you what to do. Understood?"

Sully nodded. "When are your other f-f-friends getting here?" he asked.

"My friends?"

He gestured at the empty seats.

She stared at him with narrowed eyes. "I'm fixin' to exercise rule number one. So why don't you keep your trap shut until the bell rings?"

Sully smiled to himself. He was pretty sure he and Dice would have the table to themselves.

Sully lay awake in his bare, dark room long after the house turned quiet. The room held his bed, desk, and some boxes stacked in a corner, all his things still packed away. It was too dark and too still and he felt out of place, and lonely. The first day of school had only gone downhill after lunch. He'd gotten lost on his way to geometry and was still wandering the halls after the bell rang. The teacher had not taken pity on him when he'd finally arrived. "Quite a first impression you've made, Sullahan Kildare," he'd said. "Let's see if we can arrive promptly tomorrow, shall we?" At least the kids weren't making fun of him for his stutter, yet. Nobody'd heard him talk, except Dice. No, the taunting would come later. It always did.

Thunder rumbled outside and a few drops pitter-pattered against the window. Then the rain came harder, growing in intensity until it seemed lakes and oceans of water must be coming down. A low thump sounded from somewhere behind his head. He looked back, startled, but nothing was there. Thunder, surely? No, there it was again. From inside the wall. Not too loud, like somebody had weakly pounded a fist.

He put his head on his pillow and tried to remember the layout of the house. It was a lot bigger than anyplace they'd lived before. The next room over was the guest room. Shouldn't be anybody in there. He looked at the digital clock but it was dark. The power must have gone out. It'd been a little past midnight the last time he'd looked so it must be about 12:30 now. *Maybe Dad is up?* Unlikely, as he had to be at his new job in the morning. And anyway, why hadn't he heard him in the hallway?

Another thump, a little louder now, and directly behind him. His heart was beating fast and he hardly dared move. His mind raced, trying to reason out what could be making the sound. *Not mice. Maybe a raccoon.*

He strained his ears, and thought he could make something out. It was hard to tell with the sound of the rain on the window, but it sounded almost like…whispering. Yes, whispering, from inside the wall. And another thump, there was no mistaking it now. Whatever was in there, it was no raccoon.

He strained to make out the words but it was impossible with the noise from the storm covering it up. For a moment the rain let up and in the interlude he heard one word through the wall, distinct and clear: "Sullahan."

He pulled the sheets over his head and curled his body up. He was shivering though it wasn't cold, and every sense now was acutely tuned. But after the whisper there were no more sounds that night. He was sure of that, for he was awake every moment of it. And in the morning, the overturned box he was using as a bedside table was bare. The triskelion was gone.

# CHAPTER TWO

Sully sat at the breakfast table, bleary-eyed, spooning Cheerios to his mouth. He'd spent an hour crawling under beds, sticking his fingers in cracks under the baseboard, and moving unopened boxes in search of the triskelion, but it was truly missing.

Still, the world seemed a lot less menacing in the daytime. The kitchen windows weren't yet dressed with curtains or blinds and bright morning sunlight illuminated countless dust motes floating in and out of the shafts of light. It made the kitchen look like an aquarium, millions of tiny creatures drifting around him, the table, the stacks of unpacked boxes. Sully's father came in wearing khakis and a blazer, his big stomach straining against his buttoned-down dress shirt, a whale disrupting the currents as the plankton parted around his form.

"You ready for school?" the whale asked in his gravelly voice.

"Yeah." Sully continued spooning his cereal without looking up.

"Good." Sully's dad poured himself a cup from the coffee maker and added cream and sugar. "I want you to work hard here. Try an' do better than Murfreesboro. This is a fresh start for you. Teachers don't know nothin' about you." His dad paused but Sully didn't speak. He went on, a little harsher this time. "I mean it, boy, you best watch yourself."

"R-right," Sully answered. Had to say something to get his father to stop talking.

His dad leaned against a counter and sipped from his mug while looking out across the broad lawn lined with dogwoods. He fingered the knot of his tie self-consciously. He was used to work boots and a uniform, not these clothes. "We got a deal on this place, Sullahan. If my job works out, we could live in Moorestown a long time."

"Dad?"

"Yeah?"

"I heard s-something in the walls last night. L-like something crawling in there."

His dad drained the coffee and put the mug in the sink. "Probably mice or rats. Not too surprisin' in an old house like this. I'll call the exterminator today."

"I d-don't think it was mice," Sully said.

"How would you know? You a mouse expert now?" His dad's voice was louder and edged with irritation. Sully never knew what would set his father off lately. He shrank himself down in his seat while his dad ranted. "You don't think it's mice? I don't care if it's squirrels or rabbits or South American crocodiles, we're getting' rid of 'em. Stop worryin' about it and go finish gettin' ready."

"Yes, sir," Sully said, slipping out before the whale got any angrier. He had the feeling without the triskelion, his bad luck was going to get even worse.

---

Dice's table was occupied by others, and there was no sign of her anywhere. *Maybe she's sick. Or in the principal's office.* No matter, he'd have to find someplace else. He wandered the cafeteria, squeezing between chairs and tables while trying to appear inconspicuous. The lunchroom was always the worst part of any new school.

13

In class, you could sit in your desk and stay quiet, but at lunch you had to find a seat.

Finally, he spotted a table with a couple older kids seated at it, tenth-graders he judged, and several empty seats. Not ideal, but pretty much the only choice. He approached with trepidation, putting down his tray when neither of the boys said anything. One boy was dressed completely in camouflage, his blond hair cut close to his scalp. The other wore a black t-shirt with a skull and crossbones and curled his upper lip, showing off the sparse dark hairs that were grown just thick enough to be called a mustache. They both had several inches and many pounds on Sully.

"You're new here, ain't you?" said the blond one.

"Yeah," Sully said, hoping he sounded tough. He tried to open his milk but he was kind of nervous and tore the cardboard spout.

"Ha! How you gon' drink that now?" said the dark-haired one.

"G-guess I'll g-get a straw," Sully said, though he didn't really want to leave his food with these two. But if he took his tray with him, he might lose his seat.

"Naw, you ain't got to do that. You jes' got to use blowjob lips, like Tommy here," the blond one said. The other boy, apparently Tommy, grinned and formed his lips into an O, pouring his milk into his mouth. A little bit dribbled down his chin. "Aw, you spilled some, Tommy."

Sully was feeling distinctly uncomfortable with this conversation. He took a look around the cafeteria to see if Dice might have come in.

"What's the matter? You don't want to sit with us?" the blond one asked.

"He lookin' for his friend, Camo Boy," Tommy said in a tone of voice that suggested he wasn't the brains of the duo.

"Yeah, that right? Who's your friend, new kid?" Camo Boy asked.

Sully shrugged and didn't say a word.

"He Dice's friend," Tommy said. "I seen 'em sittin' together."

Camo Boy let out a low whistle. "Dice's friend, huh? She weird, man. Didn't know she had friends." He leaned over conspiratorially and stage-whispered to Sully. "So, you gettin' some o' that?"

"Wh-what?" Sully said.

"I mean, are you hittin' that?" he said, louder. "Bangin' it? You know, givin' it to her with her pants off?" Tommy snorted and guffawed at Camo Boy's witticism.

Sully shoveled in a last forkful of meatloaf and stood. There was still food left on his plate but he didn't feel hungry any more. He headed to the trash can.

"Hey, was it somethin' I said?" Camo Boy called after him. "Tell your girlfriend I said hi!"

---

Sully walked home from school a different way, just to see the neighborhood. The air in this town smelled different than the last one, humid and salty. His dad had told him Moorestown was near the beach, but they hadn't been yet. The roads were quiet, and only a few people were out, raking or working on their cars. Loblolly pines soared in yards, gray lumpy-barked trunks rising fifty feet, yellow-green needles in the sky. Pine straw and pinecones littered the grass.

He turned onto a road that intersected with his own. A white panel van with *Jim's Pest Control Service* written on the side was parked at the end of the street, right around the corner from the house. Good. Maybe the raccoons, or whatever, would be gone that night. Then he could look for the triskelion. Not to mention get some sleep. He'd been exhausted all day.

Nobody was home so Sully opened the front door

with the spare key in his backpack. That was no surprise. His dad had to work late here, selling cars until long after dinnertime. Strange he didn't see the exterminator anywhere, though. *Must be in his truck doing paperwork or something.*

At least he had the house to himself for a couple hours. After his mom had left, being in an empty house alone had frightened him, but he'd grown out of that. He thought about looking for the triskelion some more, but the next step would be searching inside the walls, and he wasn't sure where to even begin with that.

Instead he went to his room and unstacked a few boxes until he found a small one he'd packed especially. He ripped the tape off, opened the flaps, tipped it over on his bed. Out spilled a heap of stopped watches, busted calculators, disassembled stereos and radios, wires and circuits and screws and washers and metal bits and a few tools. "Why are you packin' all that crap?" his dad had asked him back in Tennessee. Sully, afraid he'd throw it out, had waited until his father was asleep before carefully, quietly arranging it all in the box and sealing it.

He rummaged through the parts, enjoying the happy clinking sound they made when he stirred his hand in the pile. Without looking his fingers found the round tube he was searching for: a broken pen, black and elegant but quite useless. From his pocket he pulled a tiny spring he'd spotted on the ground that day. He unscrewed the body and slid the spring in. The fit was perfect. He screwed it all back together and pushed in the top with his thumb. It popped with a satisfying click and the pen nub locked into place. At his desk he wrote out his signature on a piece of notebook paper. The pen wrote beautifully. *Why can't all the other problems in my life be fixed so easily?*

# CHAPTER THREE

Moorestown High School was a giant brick heap, five stories tall, built decades before and never renovated since. A high wrought-iron fence surrounded the grounds, which were littered with junk food wrappers, soft drink cans, and shards of glass. Graffiti covered its walls, "D & R" written in big bubble letters on the wall facing the basketball courts. This was where the athletic boys shot hoops before the bell and the cool girls gossiped on the sidelines, while the less popular kids clustered around the edges of the blacktop on the packed, grassless earth, staring at their phones. *Like planets around a sun,* thought Sully.

And if they were planets, he must be a comet, flying through the vacuum of space, destined to pass eternally around the other celestial bodies but never meeting them. Or so it seemed to him as he trudged around the school, unnoticed and too timid to approach kids he didn't know. His head ached and his body dragged. The voices had been back, and he'd passed another night without sleep. They were saying his name more often now.

On his third pass around the schoolyard he spotted Dice under a magnolia over in the corner, the only bit of green in the whole place. Actually, she was circling the tree, running her fingers over its knobby trunk while walking around it repeatedly, a little girl's pink backpack slung over her shoulder and clanking loudly as she walked. *What could she possibly have in there?* As he approached, he could hear her singing softly.

"My f-fellow comet," Sully said, smiling. He didn't expect her to get it, of course. He'd have to explain the joke. But what he really didn't expect her to do was scream like she'd seen a ghost, which is what she did. His smile flattened while nearby kids stopped talking and turned to stare.

"You shouldn't sneak up on people like that," she said far too loudly. "You scared the hell out of me."

"I'm s-s-s-"

"Sorry, yeah, I know."

The kids nearby went back to their conversations. She went back to circling the tree and singing. As if in orbit, Sully thought. Maybe Dice wasn't a comet like him. Maybe she was more like a satellite, revolving around a world and broadcasting a song no one had the antenna to receive.

"I didn't s-see you yesterday," Sully said. When Dice failed to respond, he added, "In the cafeteria, I m-mean."

"Yeah. Sometimes I leave early."

"Really? Where do you g-go?" Sully asked.

Dice shot him in irritated look. "What are you doing here, anyway?"

He wasn't sure what she meant. Where else would he be before school? "I thought m-maybe I could s-stand with you."

Dice let out an exaggerated sigh. "Look, I let you eat lunch with me because I felt sorry for you, all right? It doesn't mean we're BFFs. As you can see, I'm in the middle of something."

Sully couldn't see that at all, but he didn't want to say it. He felt a little panicked. He definitely did not want to risk antagonizing her and having to sit God knows where at lunch. What to say, what to say? He patted his pocket and felt the pen in it. That might interest her. "L-look," he said, pulling it out and holding it out to her. "I f-f-fixed this."

"Oh, a gift for me?" Dice said. Sully lowered his brow; he hadn't really meant to give it away. Still, he didn't withdraw his hand and Dice took it from him. She inspected it, giving it a trial click. "I might let you stand near me, after all."

"Gee, th-thanks."

"You ain't got to look so down," she said to him as she slipped the pen into her backpack. "I got something for you too."

"You do?"

"Sure I do. My sparkling personality, of course." She eyed his shirt. "Hey, where's your good luck charm?"

"It's g-gone. I think somebody took it."

"Who?"

Should he tell her the truth? Why not? "Th-there are things living in m-my walls at home." Sully knew how it must sound but Dice didn't even blink.

The bell rang. "See you at lunch?" Sully asked.

"Maybe, maybe not." She sauntered off with a sing-song "Ta-ta." Sully turned, bewildered, to go to class. Camo Boy had been right about one thing: Dice was weird.

After lunch, the clock in the math classroom ticked the seconds away with all the urgency of an old lady crossing the street. Sully's eyes drooped lower and lower. He'd been two nights without sleep and his body thought this would be the perfect place to catch up. Geometry class receded and his muscles relaxed. Behind him somebody dropped a pencil, the sound as it hit the floor jarring him to attention, his head swinging up with a snap and an involuntary gasp. Mr. Clarence interrupted his lecture on finding the area of a polygon to shoot him a derisive glance.

Sully paid rapt attention for about two minutes but felt himself fading. It was no good. He would never be able to pay attention in this condition. Maybe a walk would help. He didn't like to speak out in class, but it was that or nod off again.

"Mr. Clarence," he said, raising his hand.

"Yes, Sullahan?"

"Can I g-go to the restroom?"

"You mean, may I go to the restroom."

Now everybody's eyes were on him, which made him nervous. "M-m-may—"

"Yeess?" Mr. Clarence said.

"M-m-may I g-g-go to the r-restroom?"

"Why yes, you may." Mr. Clarence gave him a little smirk and the class laughed. "Don't forget to take the hall pass with you."

He could hear the comments as he hurried out the door. "It took him long enough." "I'm surprised he didn't pee his pants before he got it out." So, it was beginning already. Well, it was inevitable. The mocking would follow, then the outright bullying. *Same here as anywhere.*

The hallway was quiet, the only sound the droning of teachers from the open classroom doors he passed. The bathroom smelled smoky but seemed unoccupied. At the sink he splashed cold water on his face. In the scratched and pitted mirror he saw a stall door open behind him, releasing a cloud of smoke and a tall figure. Black heavy metal t-shirt. Scraggly mustache.

"Hey, Camo Boy, look who's here!" Tommy called out.

Sully whirled around just in time to see the next stall door open. Out came Camo Boy in a similar cloud of smoke, one hand behind his back.

"If it ain't Dice's boyfriend," Camo Boy said. He let his hand fall to his side, a cigarette nestled between two fingers. "I don't reckon you gonna tell nobody what we doin' in here, are you?"

"I d-don't talk much," Sully said. Cold water dripped from his face onto his shirt but he decided to forget the paper towels. He took one step toward the exit instead.

"Not so fast, new kid," Camo Boy said. Tommy blocked the door and Camo Boy sidled right up until his chin was almost touching Sully's forehead. Sully breathed in the gray, faintly metallic smell of cigarette smoke on Camo Boy's shirt. "Your lunch money," he demanded.

"I already ate l-lunch," Sully said. "We have the s-same l-lunch period."

That confused Camo Boy for a moment, but he recovered quickly. "Your pockets," he said. "Empty 'em. Everything you got."

Sully pulled out the contents of his pockets and put them in Camo Boy's sweaty, outstretched hand. A pencil stub. A dime. A bubblegum wrapper Dice had given him in the cafeteria and said to throw away for her.

"That it?" Camo Boy said.

"Y-yes." Sully's mouth was dry. "Th-that's it." That wasn't it. He knew it and Camo Boy knew it.

The older boy reached down and put his hand into the pocket of Sully's corduroys. It occurred to Sully that if he were slicker, he could make some comment about Camo Boy at this moment. *Hey, you trying to cop a feel?* A well-placed remark could change the situation around, maybe even turn Tommy against him. Dice would cut them to ribbons with her words, if she were here. But he wasn't slick, words weren't his friends, and he didn't say a thing.

Camo Boy pulled out a watch, holding it like a worm he'd fished out of compost. Silver and crystal glittered in the hazy light of the boys' restroom. "A lady's watch?" he said.

"Please," Sully said. His eyes teared up. First losing the triskelion, now his mom's watch.

Tommy had abandoned his post to take a better look at the booty. "Looks fancy, Camo Boy."

Camo Boy peered at the watch face. "It don't work though." He thumped it once. "Nope, dead."

"I haven't fixed it yet," Sully whispered.

Camo Boy looked back up at him. "Yeah, thanks, new kid. This'll do."

Sully wanted to protest, wanted to punch them right in their tenth-grade faces, but he didn't. He just stood. Tommy shoved him roughly out the door. Sully glared at the restroom with red-rimmed eyes before plodding, defeated, back to class.

# CHAPTER FOUR

Sully sensed somebody following him. His body stiffened, his perceptions heightened. He didn't stop though, so as not to alert his pursuer. From the corner of his eye he could see a figure running around trees and ducking behind fences, though every time he turned no one was there. *Jesus, wasn't the watch enough?* Maybe he should run for it, get home quick as possible, lock the door behind him. Then again, he wasn't sure he wanted Camo Boy and Tommy to know where he lived. With a more circuitous route he might be able to elude them. Or perhaps they would lose interest after a while.

He decided on the long way home. He marched fast and stuck to the middle of the road so he could spot anybody approaching. Finally, out of breath and sweat running down his cheeks, he rounded the corner to his own street, pretty sure he'd lost them. The white panel van was still there, parked in the exact same place it had been yesterday. Odd. Maybe the exterminator hadn't finished the job. But wouldn't he have parked in a different spot if he'd left and come back? Anyway, Sully was less than confident the exterminator would be able to kill whatever was in the walls.

"Hey, what're you lookin' at, kid?" came a voice from a nearby bush.

Sully relaxed. "Oh, it's y-you," he called. A branch quivered. "You c-can come out, Dice. I kn-know it's you."

Dice popped out with a grin on her face and leaves in her hair. "Had you goin' there for a little while, didn't I?"

"Yeah," Sully admitted.

"So how'd you figure out it was me?" she asked.

Sully gave her a look. "I'm a s-stutterer, not an idiot."

"Uh huh," she said. "What's the deal here? Is this your house or what?"

"Th-this is it on the corner."

"C'mon, let's look for your good luck charm," Dice said, already headed past the line of dogwoods along the property line.

Sully didn't refuse, but didn't feel too hopeful about the prospects. In any case, Dice seemed less concerned with finding the triskelion than with poking around all the overgrown landmarks hidden beneath layers of choking kudzu. It must have been years since anybody had done any work in the yard. Sully kept a step behind her as she peeked in the rusty shed in the corner, kept her balance on a giant fallen oak, tugged at an ornate iron portal to the crawlspace under the house that wouldn't open.

"What are you d-doing, anyway?" Sully asked after a few minutes.

"Y'all's place sure is big," she said, checking around to see if she'd missed anything interesting. "No sign of your charm out here. Let's see if it's inside."

"I'm not s-supposed to let anybody in the house if my d-dad isn't home," Sully said.

"Fine. I'll wait." She plopped down on a pile of leaves. "Bring me back a snack."

In the house there were only empty boxes and eerie quiet. He'd never noticed before how lonely the house was without another person there. He checked the refrigerator and the pantry. Not much available. His dad wasn't much of a shopper. He found an apple on the counter, cut it up, and went back out.

Dice called to him from behind some huge overgrown boxwoods near the air conditioning unit. She had returned to the crawlspace door. It was made of wrought iron and ornately decorated with an engraved flower pattern, placed at about knee-level. Seemed like a lot of effort to put into such a functional part of the house.

"Look," she said. "I think I know where your charm might have gone."

"What, in there? D-did you get it open?" he asked, handing her the apple slices.

"No, look on the ground." She popped one in her mouth and indicated a bare patch in the lawn just in front of the door. He peered at the spot. The soil was loose, as if it'd been recently dug up. He raked away dirt with his hands while Dice stood and chewed. He felt something metal, dug away more dirt until he could pull it out. It was a padlock.

"I bet th-that was for this door," Sully said. He felt a surge of hope. If the padlock was on the ground, somebody might have been in here lately. Somebody with the triskelion.

"But we couldn't open it before, genius, and the padlock was off then," Dice said. "Why would it need a padlock if it's jammed?"

Sully inspected the crawlspace door. "Here's why it w-won't open," he said. "The latch is all twisted." He pulled on it but it didn't budge. "I could g-go get my tools."

"Stand back," Dice said. She gave the latch a donkey kick and the door swung out with a creak. "That's how you do it." She peered in and gasped.

"Wh-what is it?" Sully asked.

She pulled out a white ballcap and held it up. The logo read *Jim's Pest Control Service.*

"The exterminator! Th-that's why his truck's still there. M-maybe he went in and got stuck."

"Or lost," Dice added. She got on her hands and knees and stuck her head in.

"What do you see?" Sully asked.

"Nothin', it's dark. Duh." She crawled in without hesitation.

"Wh-what are you doing?" Sully called after her, grabbing for but missing her white tennis shoe as it disappeared. "Are you c-crazy?"

She laughed and called out. "What, you want to leave the poor guy in here? He could be trapped somewhere. Maybe he saw your charm."

Sully wondered if this wouldn't be a good time to

explain to her about the voices and what exactly might be in the walls. No time, though, she was already well inside. "I don't think this is a good idea," he said. "Shouldn't we go get a flashlight, at least?"

"Come on, you big wuss," came the reply.

*If there is something in there, I can't let her go by herself.* Despite a heartbeat like a snare drum and a tightening in his stomach, Sully dropped to all fours and went in after her. She was already halfway under the house, and he scrambled after her across the cold dirt and between cinderblock pilings. The light behind them grew distant and the way narrowed as they advanced. After a point the ground sloped downward and the walls and ceiling tapered. It seemed to Sully that they must have crawled much farther than the length of the house. When the light faded away entirely Sully followed by listening to the sounds of Dice's hands and knees brushing along the dirt. He wanted to protest, but his throat was so clogged up he couldn't get a sentence out.

And then he heard the whispers, like at night in his bed, too quiet to make out the words but getting closer and louder. This spurred his mouth to working: "D-dice, let's g-go back. I d-d-don't like it."

The brushing sound ahead of him stopped. "Yeah,

maybe you're right." Her voice carried back, tinged with alarm. "We could go get that flashlight you were talking about."

Sully tried to turn himself around but found the passage much narrower than he had expected. He really had to tuck his body into a ball to turn. The whispering grew louder and closer.

"What's taking so long?" Dice asked, the panic in her voice rising. He felt her pressing against him which only made his contortions more difficult. "Hurry!"

"I'm t-t-trying to!" he said. "M-my leg's stuck!"

"Hurry faster, you stuttering fool!" she yelled, the whispers now much closer, so close it was possible to distinguish several separate voices.

Dice screamed and at the same time something grabbed him. Lots of somethings, holding his arms and legs and pulling him down the passage. It felt like hands, only the fingers had a chill that spread across his skin and into the interior of his body. He struggled, throwing his elbows and kicking his feet wherever he felt himself being held, but it was as if whatever he was striking was no more than vapor, wafting away as soon as he touched it. In the end, there were too many hands, if that's what they were, and they pulled him deeper and deeper.

He gave up struggling. He could hear Dice ahead, screaming and cursing, but he himself stayed still and concentrated on the whispering. Sometimes he heard names, different names, including his own, but he couldn't understand most of the words in between.

At one point he felt himself being lowered as if down a shaft, and he was overcome by queasiness. "I can't see!" he shouted out.

The answer came back in dozens or hundreds of whispers, now in perfect English. "He can't see! He can't see! You have the solution for that, don't you! Yes, yes, go get the solution! Oh, he will see!" And then whispery laughter. He felt himself laid on the ground, and a sort of cold wet jelly was pressed in his eyes. He shrieked and screwed his eyelids closed as tight as he could make them.

"Open them! Yes, open them and see!" came the whispers all around him. Slowly, tentatively, Sully did as they said, and when he opened his eyes he found he could perceive his surroundings perfectly.

# PART TWO:
# DICE

# CHAPTER FIVE

Sully gazed in every direction, trying to find his bearings. All was dim and silvery, as on a moonlit night. He found he was in a pit, rough-hewn and shallow. It should be easy to climb out. Still, he felt queasy and decided to sit for a while, hoping the feeling would pass. All around the pit walls and across the dirt floor swirled dark shapes, like people but all flat and stretched out.

"He sees! Oh yes, he sees!" whispered the shapes. "How does he like it? Not sure yet, is he? Give him time, give him time! He will learn to like it, yes! See things he will! All sorts of things! Stay with us he will."

A moaning came from a dark corner. Dice. She was lying in the fetal position and Sully couldn't tell if she was injured. He crawled to her and put his hand on her arm.

"Dice," he said. No answer. "Dice!"

"Sully? Is that you?" Her voice was slurred, as if she wasn't fully awake.

"Yes. Are you okay?"

"I don't know," she mumbled.

He examined her. There didn't seem to be any blood or anything, but that didn't mean she wasn't hurt. He still felt nauseated, but ignored it. More important to get Dice out of this place, if he could.

"I'm going," he said out loud, though he wasn't sure whom he was talking to. The shapes passed all around them, gliding, insubstantial, not even stirring the air. "And I'm taking her with me."

"He's taking her, he's taking her," came the whispers. "Leaving? We gave him a gift and now he leaves! The Queen will be displeased."

Sully had no idea what any of that that meant and he didn't intend to stick around to inquire further. He took Dice's hand but her arm was limp. He gave her a shake to try to wake her up. She groaned and rolled away from him. He lifted her from her armpits and with some trouble pushed her body up over the lip of the pit.

He climbed up after her and found they were in a large earthen chamber. Tree roots dangled from the ceiling and numerous passageways branched off. He wasn't sure which way to go, or how he was going to drag Dice all the way back to the surface.

The shapes continued to circle him, the exact number impossible to fix. Dozens, at least, maybe hundreds, intertwined and continually moving and passing over and under each other like eels in a bucket.

"Which way do I go?" he asked. Raspy laughter came from all around him. Not too helpful. But the eel image gave him an idea.

He squatted, readied his hand, and when the moment came, snapped one up in a flash. The shape struggled and hissed. It was cold and slippery, though not wet. Actually, it was not quite solid, almost like holding a piece of fog, but he held on and squeezed tight.

Sully snarled in the meanest voice he could muster. "You show me the way out, and I'll let you go."

"Yes, yes, whatever you want," the thing cried in a pitiful voice.

"And tell the others to carry my friend," Sully added.

"Do it! Do it!" it called out. Dice's body rose in the air as if levitated.

"Good, let's go," Sully commanded.

Sully's captive led him along a maze of paths

impossible to remember. "Left… right here and around the bend… now left again where the passage splits off," it said, while the other shapes carried Dice along behind. As they ascended she murmured and stirred, gradually awakening.

After a time they reached a tunnel where the ceiling and walls closed in, and Sully had to crawl forward on hands and knees.

"Here we are, yes," the thing said. "Under the house. Your door up ahead."

Sully could feel cool outside air blow in gently, fresh after the stale underground atmosphere. The shape whimpered and Sully opened his hand. It leaped out and glided back down the passage with its mates, eels retreating into their hole. Dice opened her eyes.

"Oh, God! I must have fallen asleep," she said.

"How do you feel?"

"Strange," Dice said. "How long have we been under here?"

"I'm not sure," Sully said. "But we're going now." He smiled to himself. She was fine. They crawled out and found it was nighttime. In the house lights were on and he could see his father in the kitchen, pacing and smoking with a cell phone pressed to his ear. He had some trepidation about going in. The only question was how angry his dad would be.

---

Sully's dad pulled his Chevy Silverado up in front of a two-story brick house with arched windows, a wrap-around front porch, and Tuscan columns supporting the roof. Dice's house, on an elegant street in the heart of Moorestown's historic district.

His dad stepped out and glanced around uneasily. Not the kind of neighborhood where he fit in. Dice herself fell oddly silent, after chattering to them both the whole drive over. The three stood on the front porch and Sully's dad pushed the doorbell, producing a symphony of bells from somewhere in the house. A stone over the arched doorway had a simple inscription: 1854. Not the address, Sully realized. The year it was built.

A tall, elegant dark-skinned woman answered the front door, wearing a white dress and high heels even at this late hour. "You must be Mr. Kildare," she said with a smile that did not seem genuine. "Come right in."

They followed her into the sumptuously furnished front hall. Pink marble floor covered with a thick Persian rug, bronze-framed mirrors, glass display cases, dark wood sideboards. Was the woman Dice's mom? If so, she didn't hug her or touch her daughter, or even acknowledge she was there.

A plump man in a tuxedo entered through a swinging door at the far end of the hall. "So," he said in a booming voice as he approached, "you're the one who found our wayward daughter. Sorry we weren't home when you called earlier. Benefit dinners always run late, you know."

"Yeah, well, it was my boy who found her," Sully's dad said, eyes darting around. "From what I can make of his story, he was with her the whole time."

"Very good, very good," Dice's dad said indifferently. He didn't bother looking at Dice but carried on talking with Sully's dad. "You're new to the area, aren't you, Mr. Kildare?"

Sully and Dice stood and fidgeted while the grown-ups chatted. Sully was trying to figure her parents out. Dice's folks didn't seem to care she'd even been gone. His own dad had called the police and set neighbors to searching. True, he was pissed. Sully knew he was in for it later. But at least his dad had *noticed*.

While he was thinking this through, he saw Dice creep away. She squeezed around the adults, approaching a table. On top of it stood a clock, blue enamel and silver around the edges. Sully guessed it was pretty old, maybe even out of the nineteenth century. She lifted her hand and he knew exactly what she was going to do.

"No!" he called out, but it was too late. The clock fell and broke into pieces, gears and shards of glass skipping across the floor.

"Eurydice Brown!" her mother said coldly. "How dare you!"

"Sorry, Mother," Dice said, not sounding it at all. "My hand just slipped."

"It did no such thing," her mother said. "John, go get a broom or something to clean this up."

"Yes, dear," Dice's dad said, disappearing back behind the swinging door.

"Do you have any idea how much this is worth?" Dice's mom said. Now she looked at her daughter, her eyes burning. "This was an Austrian carriage clock!"

"So order another one," Dice said. "Nobody cares about that shit anyway."

"Don't you bring that ghetto talk in this house, young lady!" Her eyes bulged so wide with anger Sully thought she might have a brain aneurysm right there.

Dice's dad returned with a broom, dustpan, and plastic shopping bag.

43

"Now you help clean this up," Dice's mother said. Dice took a step back and folded her arms across her chest.

"I'll help," Sully said, hoping to defuse the tension. He bent down and held the dustpan while Dice's dad swept the fragments onto it.

"I'll take this to the jeweler tomorrow, Angela," Dice's dad said, tying the ends of the bag together. "I don't think he'll be able to do much with it, though."

"I'll fix it," Sully said. All the adults got quiet.

"What are you talkin' about, boy?" Sully's dad finally said. "That ain't one of your broken wristwatches."

"It's almost the same," Sully said. "I can do it."

Dice's dad handed Sully the bag. "Be my guest, son," he said. Dice's mom gripped her husband's forearm and glanced at Sully, opened her mouth to speak, but her dad raised his hand to shush her. "Bring it back when it's ready."

---

That night, Sully lay in bed. His dad hadn't yelled or threatened or anything after they came home. In fact, he'd surprised Sully.

"I know things ain't been easy for you," he'd said,

quietly placing a hand on Sully's shoulder. Sully had wanted to say something back, but wasn't sure what. Maybe his father had felt the same way. He'd opened his mouth, closed it, leaned over and tousled Sully's hair. "It's pretty late. We'll talk in the mornin'."

The house now was quiet, no whispers from the walls or much of any other sound either. Sully was exhausted but for some reason sleep was slow to come. Suddenly he sat up straight, wide awake. He'd just realized something: he hadn't stuttered a bit at Dice's house. His stutter was gone.

# CHAPTER SIX

The morning arrived wet and pencil lead gray, an icy drizzle falling in the cold air. Sully trudged past the empty, graffiti-covered storefronts and cracked parking lots on the way to school. The fog was so heavy he heard the thick sloshing of tires on the road long before he saw approaching cars, and even then could only make out the faint glow of headlights in the mist. He felt alone, more so than usual, as if the world was dead and only he was left.

At a corner he came upon a man, almost stumbled on him in the fog. "Excuse me," Sully mumbled but the man didn't respond. He wore a trench coat and an old-fashioned fedora. His head was tilted as if he heard something. The high school was down the street, maybe he was listening to the subdued voices of the teens waiting for the bell to ring, little more than a murmur at this distance.

The man's head, no more than a few inches from Sully's own, slowly turned and the boy shivered on seeing his face. His skin was blue and hairless and no nose protruded, in its place a flat space with two holes. His eyes were unnaturally large, the irises the same pale blue as the skin, and they regarded Sully without blinking. Sully tried to speak, scream, something, anything. His mouth was dry and no words formed, only a gasping, choking sound.

The man grinned, revealing behind his dark blue lips a row of sharp, dog-like teeth. "Good morning, Sullahan," he said. His breath, cold rot and bone marrow, wafted in Sully's face. "Be seeing you around." And the blue man tipped his hat and strode off down the street until he vanished in the fog.

Sully was frozen to the spot and it was several minutes before he dared advance. When he did it was at top speed, covering the last block to school in record time. Never was he happier to go through the front gate, relief coming with the sound of the morning bell.

In the school building, everything had a washed-out look, like the humming fluorescent lights were turned too bright. Lockers grated and squealed when kids pushed the doors into their ill-fitting metal frames, and the buzzes and creaks and cracks of the ancient building were headache-inducingly loud. Sully wondered if he were feverish. He didn't feel bad though, just a little out of sorts.

Despite losing his stutter, Sully spoke no more that day than he did any other day, which is to say, not at all. Mostly it was a matter of habit, though it wasn't as if he had any friends to talk with anyway. Today his mind was too preoccupied with the incidents of the day before to listen to the normal prattling of his classmates, discussing their plans for the weekend or the latest video games. What he really wanted to do was talk things over with Dice, see what she remembered, what her impressions were. Finally lunchtime rolled around.

"What've you got?' he asked Dice as soon as he sat at their table.

"Peanut butter and potato chip," she said. "The usual."

"Oh, gross," Sully said. "You're going to eat that?"

"Of course," Dice said. "You're just jealous 'cause

48

your lunch is so boring. And also, what happened to your stutter?"

"Gone, I guess. Since yesterday." Sully took a bite and chewed his bologna. "So how'd it go? With your parents?"

"You saw how it went," she said, and tapped her fingers on the table.

He had the feeling this topic annoyed her and she was about to invoke one of her rules. He wondered if it was always like that, if her parents ever paid attention to her, but he wasn't sure how to put it without getting kicked out of his seat. Time to change the subject. "So, what do you think those things were that grabbed us?"

"Somebody grabbed you, new kid?" came a voice from behind him. "Sure they weren't just tryin' to touch your ass?" Two trays slid onto the table from opposite directions: Camo Boy and Tommy. Sully sighed and looked at the ceiling.

"Nuh uh," Dice said. "Y'all got to find another place."

"Ain't no other place," Camo Boy said. "And I don't see your name on these seats, anyhow."

"I ain't got to put my name on 'em, 'cause I'll put an imprint of my fist on your face if you don't get up right now."

"Aw, come on, Dice," Camo Boy said. "We got nowhere else to sit. We won't hurt nuthin'."

Dice glared at them but they ignored her and started eating. Tommy took his piece of pizza, rolled it up like a carpet, and inserted the entire thing in his gaping mouth. Cheese and pizza sauce dribbled down his chin.

"Oh, my God," Dice said.

"So," Camo Boy said to Sully, "you ever get in Dice's pants like you told us you would?"

Sully didn't respond, just stared at him. There was a slow fade of something like melting silver across his vision.

Camo Boy actually felt a little uncomfortable. "Sumpin' wrong? Why you lookin' at me all freaky?"

As Camo Boy talked, his face grew older, turning tanned and weather-beaten, wrinkles around his eyes. His eyes were bloodshot and a cigarette hung from his mouth, a putrid stink of wine emanating from his mouth and clothes. Sully blinked and turned his gaze to Tommy. Tommy too transformed in front of him, his flesh spreading and bloating until an enormous gut hung over his pants, his hair thinned and greasy, fat fingers waving in the air.

Sully shook his head and screwed his eyes closed.

When he opened them Camo Boy and Tommy were back to normal. Well, as normal as they ever were. Geez, maybe he really was getting sick. "Gotta get some air," Sully muttered, backing up. His chair fell over when he stood but he didn't bother picking it up.

"Hey, don't leave yet," Camo Boy said. "You ain't even told us if Dice likes it doggy-style!" Tommy laughed so hard he spewed chunks of half-chewed pizza across the table.

Sully edged through the crowd in the cafeteria, ducked into the boys' room and leaned against the wall. What was going on? Why had they changed in front of his eyes? It must be an illusion or something, because nobody else seemed to have noticed.

He splashed water on his face, shook his head as if doing so could clear the images from his mind. It didn't work. As he leaned with his elbows on the sink, he heard a muffled clanking in the hallway. He didn't have to see to know that sound: Dice's backpack. *Good. Maybe I'll get a chance to talk to her without the two morons.* He made it out to the hallway just in time to see her slipping out the door to the blacktop. No need to bother going back in the cafeteria. He hiked up his own backpack on his shoulder and followed her.

He expected her to head to the magnolia tree she circled in the mornings, but she wasn't there when he exited. *Strange. Where could she have gone?* There—he caught a glimpse of her hot pink backpack disappearing around the back of the school building. That was an off-limits area. He wasn't sure why she'd be interested in the dumpsters and loading dock back there, but this could be even better than the conversation he'd hoped to have. He might finally be able to learn the mystery of where she vanished those days she wasn't at lunch.

He looked around. No teachers.

As he turned the corner he caught sight of a figure running into the wooded area across the service driveway behind the school. No time to hesitate, if he didn't go now she'd be gone. He took off at a run, out the gate, into the trees, tripping and sliding down a small vine-covered ravine where he thought he'd seen her go. By the time he reached bottom his pants were soaked but he couldn't stop now. She headed towards an old industrial part of town, near the river, darting through empty lots and trash-strewn alleys. There were a couple times he almost lost her, but even when he couldn't see her he followed the clanking noise.

Her destination was the rear of an old brick warehouse

at the bottom of a weedy hill. Sully crouched in a drainage gully worn into the hill and observed from behind a bush. She stood alone a few minutes with her hands in her pockets and her earbuds in. A slim Latino teen-ager, maybe sixteen, with an afro and thick black glasses showed up and tapped her on the shoulder. Where he came from Sully couldn't tell, he wasn't there one second and then he was. Sully strained to overhear their conversation.

"You're late," the teen-ager said.

"You're late too," Dice replied, pulling her earbuds out. "I been standing here waitin'."

"I was here before," the teen said. "You had problems?"

"Yeah," Dice replied. "A teacher saw me tryin' to leave."

"You in trouble?"

"Nah, just had to wait in the lunch room 'til the coast was clear."

"Cool," he said. "You got the Spanish Montana?"

"Yeah, right in my backpack," Dice said.

Sully's eyes widened. *Spanish Montana? Are they talking about drugs?* His wet pants were riding up and he shifted stances, but it was hard to maintain his balance in such an awkward position and he tumbled over backwards. He scrambled back to his feet and peeked over the side of the gully. Dice and the teen were right in front of him.

"Sully? Are you for real?" Dice said, putting a hand to her forehead.

"A toy?" the teen said. "You brought a toy?"

"He ain't a toy. He's just a kid from school who followed me."

"Well, take him right back. We ain't doin' this shit with him around."

"Don't worry 'bout him, he's cool," Dice said.

"He cool?" the teen asked, looking Sully over skeptically. "He pasty like bread dough."

Dice gazed straight at Sully. "Believe me, he ain't gonna breathe a word."

# CHAPTER SEVEN

Dice opened her backpack, pulling down the zippers on either side until the main pouch yawned wide. Inside were a half dozen black cans with multi-colored tops. "Got one of each color," she said. "Markers too."

"Cool," the older teen said. "It's your burner, you do it."

"What is all that? What are you going to do?" Sully asked.

"You ask too many questions," Dice answered. "You two on lookout or what?"

"Yeah," the teen answered. "You hear a whistle from us and you take a hike. And don't forget no cannons. You don't leave nothin' behind, so there ain't no proof."

"Got it," Dice said.

The teen snapped his fingers and nodded his head at Sully to accompany him. They stood at the corner of the warehouse while Dice pulled a fat marker out of her backpack and outlined something on the brick wall. Sully glanced around. The silver rolldown doors of the loading docks along the side of the warehouse were all shut. Nobody here but them. In the distance the cranes of Moorestown's port rose up, bright yellow against the autumn blue sky.

The older teen looked the ninth-grader up and down, his forefinger on his chin. "Sully, huh?" the teen said.

"Yep." Sully was acutely aware that the teen was judging him at this moment, trying to decide if he could be trusted, if he really was cool enough to let in on their activities. He wondered if there was something he could say, but things always went so much worse when he tried to talk, so he kept his mouth shut.

After a minute, the teen held out his fist. "I'm Robo," he said.

Sully gave him a fist bump. He'd never done it before, but he'd seen boys at school do it between classes.

It seemed to satisfy Robo. "You should be proud of your girl," he said. "This here's her first real burner."

"Burner?" Sully shook his head.

"Yeah, you know, her first throw up that ain't just taggin her name or whatever."

"So it's graffiti," Sully said, regretting the words as soon as they left his mouth. Dumb. Why did he always have to say such dumb things?

"Yeah. It's graffiti," Robo said. "After today, Dice be a true writer."

"But isn't it illegal?"

Robo laughed. "Here," he said, taking something out of his back pocket. "Here's my black book. Take a look in there."

It was about the size of a regular notebook, with a solid black cover and thick pages. Sully thumbed through it, each new page revealing increasingly elaborate sketches. The early ones were just variations on Robo's name with different types of lettering and colors, but by the middle of the book there were pictures of weird, monstrous machine-like creatures in purple and black, writhing masses of tentacles and wires and eyeballs.

"So these are your ideas for graffiti pictures?" Sully asked.

"Not just ideas. All the ones you seen so far I already thrown up," Robo said. He raised his chin and gave an exaggerated nod like a stallion taking pride in its mane. "I

57

know you seen some of my work around town."

"I'm pretty new here," Sully said. "I've only been here a couple weeks."

"That explains it," Robo said. "Keep your eyes open. I ain't the king of Moorestown, but I'm gettin' up."

"Hey," Dice called. "I got the hollows done. You wanna come see?"

"Yeah," Robo called back. "Let's check it."

She had outlined her design across the large brick expanse. Twisty letters intricately linked and overlapped one another in an arch over a pair of dice. It took Sully a minute to figure out what the letters spelled: *Roll dem Bones.*

"Cool," Robo said, nodding. "What numbers the dice gonna show?"

"Double sixes, of course," Dice said. She pulled a couple new cans out and popped a wide nozzle tip on one. "Time for the fill."

She carefully sprayed the interior of the first letter, hot pink, the paint flowing out as brilliant as molten lava. On the brick it glowed wet and vivid. The sharp, fruity smell of acetone permeated the area. Sully stared at her work, fascinated.

Robo tapped his shoulder. "Time to get back on look

out," he said. Sully was engrossed and didn't turn his head. "You like it, yeah?"

"It's beautiful," Sully said.

"Ain't nothin' prettier," Robo replied. "Who knows, maybe one of these days we'll give you a shot."

A small lamp poured a pool of light onto the desk where all the parts of the clock lay strewn. With a Q-tip in one hand, Sully dabbed glue onto a piece of the frame; with the other hand he picked up a gear with tweezers, painstakingly placing it over a shaft. It didn't fit, though it looked like a perfect match. He bore down on it, pressing, but with too much force, and the piece broke off. His face turned angry and frustrated but he breathed deep and willed himself to calmness. With a sigh, he started over again, carefully manipulating the tiny pieces into their proper configuration.

Outside all was darkness and rain. His dad had already gone to bed and the house was quiet except for the pattering of drops on the roof. A passing car threw headlights into his room and momentarily illuminated the window. Sully glanced up and for only a split second, right outside the window, he saw it: a silhouette of a figure wearing a fedora. He screamed, or tried to, but his voice failed in his throat. The after-image faded from his retinas as darkness returned.

His inclination was to run to bed, to hide under the sheets, tuck himself away the rest of the night. But that was the easy way out. That's not what Dice would do. She would never hide. He pushed his fear down and switched off his desk lamp, so the light wouldn't reflect against the glass. Now he could see out as well as anybody outside could see in. Slowly, with his heart beating loud in his chest, he approached the window, step by step. When he looked out, there was nothing but rain falling on the grass. Whoever had been at the window was gone.

# CHAPTER EIGHT

"I'm short," Dice said to Robo. "You buy it."

Dice, Robo, and Sully loitered on the sidewalk in front of the hardware store. They were skipping school again. This time Sully had known where to look for Dice before lunch and spotted her sneaking away. When he'd joined her, she hadn't objected. Still, he knew his presence was awkward for her. He kept a step or two behind, careful not to intrude too much.

"Come on, I seen you up in that big house," Robo said. "You tellin' me Daddy don't slip you no twenties or fifties when you go out the door?"

"You're trippin'," Dice said. "My parent's won't even get me a cell phone. And I told you, I'm out. Maybe if you hadn't eaten three Big Macs you'd have somethin' left."

Robo scratched his scalp. "We'll have to rack a few cannons. And I know just the person." He tilted his head toward Sully. Sully pretended to be intensely interested in some nearby pigeons.

"No," Dice said flatly. "No way. You ain't askin' him to do that. I'll go in."

"Black girl, they gonna watch you like you in the penitentiary from the first step you take in that store," Robo said. "But our little red-headed friend, ain't nobody suspect him."

"Why don't you do it?" Dice raised her eyebrows, a challenge in her tone of voice.

"They know me here," Robo said. "Nope, won't work. It's gotta be him."

"Then we ain't gonna write today, that's all," Dice said.

"Why you defendin' him so much?" Robo's voice dropped in volume and he sidled close to Dice in mock secrecy. "This white boy got somethin' on you?"

Sully spun around, sending the pigeons fluttering. "I'll do it."

"No, you won't," Dice said. "You ain't getting in trouble 'cause Robo got no cash."

"No, I want to," Sully said. "Just tell me what to get."

"See, he cool, like you said the other day." Robo playfully punched Sully's shoulder. "He be taggin' in no time."

"Don't do this to impress me, Sully," Dice said.

"That's not why," he said. He avoided her gaze, keeping his eyes on Robo. "Tell me what I need to get."

---

Sully strolled in through the automatic door, hoping he looked nonchalant. His heartbeat was like a drum solo and he hadn't even done anything yet. He took a few deep breaths. Nobody in the store seemed to notice him.

In the paint aisle he found the shelves of spray paint, right where Robo had explained they would be. There were a lot more than he'd expected. His eyes scanned the dozens of colors marked on top of the lids. He decided to pick up just one can, glossy black. That would be useful in almost any situation, right? An older man came down the aisle and Sully almost put the can back and walked off. *Get ahold of yourself. He's just here to buy something.* The man found what he was looking for and moved on. Now the aisle was empty. This was his chance.

Sully wavered. Stealing. *Why am I doing this?* Was Dice

right, that he was trying to impress her somehow? Well, he did want to impress her, but that wasn't it. He wanted to know if he could really do it, that's all. That he had the guts to do something just because he felt like it, without worrying if anybody else cared, like Dice could. *Well? Do I have the guts to do this or not?*

Sully slid the can into his jacket, zipped it up, went down the aisle. The clerks at the checkout counters were all busy with customers. He thought he could make it out so long as nobody heard how loud his heart was thumping. He strolled through an empty lane and out the door. No alarms went off, no guards rushed and tackled him. And out on the sidewalk, Dice and Robo were waiting.

"I got it," Sully said, grinning and reaching in his jacket.

"Show us later," Robo said in a low voice. "They can still see us out the window."

"Oh, right," Sully said.

"Come on, let's get out of here," Dice said, with a frown at Sully. What did that mean? She'd been ready to steal it herself, if he hadn't done it.

They crossed the parking lot without another word, walking as fast as possible without breaking into a run.

Before they'd gotten halfway, they heard footsteps on the pavement behind them. Sully looked back. A gray-haired man with a brown apron and a nametag was charging after them.

"Oh, shit! Run!" Robo said, and they took off, through the parked cars, down the sidewalk and along a row of storefronts. One block, two blocks, Sully panting behind Robo with his long, loping stride, and Dice, surprisingly graceful and athletic. The man was shouting something at them but Sully couldn't make out his words over his own strained breathing. He didn't seem to be giving up the chase, though.

They turned a corner, Sully now falling a few steps behind. This street was more rundown and there were several boarded up buildings. Without warning, Robo jumped into one through a gaping doorway. Dice came to a sudden stop, Sully almost colliding with her as she pivoted on one foot to follow. He wheeled his arms and found his footing, stepped through the threshold behind her. Their pursuer, red-faced and huffing, was still half a block back.

It seemed to be an old church. The interior was a mess, graffiti all over the walls, with piles of lumber and fallen ceiling tiles littering the aisles between the pews.

Robo leapt over them, unconcerned with injury as he sprinted to the front in the half-darkness. He pushed open a rotten door at the side of the nave, apparently expecting it to lead outdoors but finding instead a stairway headed up. He hesitated only a moment and took the stairs two at a time.

Sully saw all this but froze. The melted silver passed over his eyes again, like it had in the cafeteria with Camo Boy and Tommy. Even as he saw Robo and Dice running, another scene now overlaid itself, also of the church. In this vision, the place was bright with fire, big timbers from the ceiling falling in, walls collapsing, the big zinc organ pipes mounted on the front wall softening and melting as the temperature rose. He looked around, seeing flames in every direction and choking black smoke filling the sanctuary.

Dice, sensing Sully had stopped, glanced back with irritation. Sure enough, that fool was standing there like a department store dummy, his eyes all weird and glazed. She bit her lip and ran back, took his hand, pulled him toward the door Robo had gone through, led him up the stairs. At the top there was a small machinery room, the space stuffed with blowers and pipes.

Robo whispered to them from a corner, "Hey, under

here." Dice yanked Sully and rolled underneath the giant pipe where Robo lay. They spoke no more but listened to the footsteps in the sanctuary below.

They heard the man downstairs stomping around, knocking things over, grunting from the exertion of getting down on his hands and knees to check under pews. When he didn't find them he called out. "I'd better not catch y'all in my store again. Next time I call the police. Y'all hear me? Next time the police!" No more noises came up the stairs after that.

"You think it's safe?" Dice whispered.

"Yeah, probably," Robo said, and rolled out. He sat up and pulled a pack of cigarettes from his jacket pocket, lit one with a lighter and sucked in. Its tip glowed bright in the dim light and its smoke cut the thick smell of dust and mildew.

"What are all these pipes and things?" Dice asked.

"For the organ, I think," Sully answered.

"Hey! What happened to you down there?" Dice demanded. "Why'd you stop? You trying to get us caught?"

"I… I thought I saw something. Kind of a vision."

"Yeah? The only vision I had was us in the back of a cop car," Dice said.

Sully didn't respond. He didn't really want to explain about it. Especially since the last thing he'd seen had been Robo, trapped by fire in the organ closet with no way out.

# CHAPTER NINE

Mr. Clarence droned on about triangle congruence, as dull as ever. Sully sat in the first row and sketched in his notebook. He might as well. With all the afternoons he'd skipped lately, he was hopelessly lost in geometry. The graffiti had revived an interest in drawing he hadn't felt since he was a little kid. He doodled across the margins of the paper, creating intricate machines, full of gears and belts, almost impossible to comprehend in their complexity but working together in a flawless whole. He imagined how perfect it would be if the whole world were like that, a beautiful machine that functioned without any parts breaking or falling out. Not like real life where, just when things started running smooth, something always jammed, some defective part popping and ruining everything and making your dad have to move, again.

Something hit the side of his head and interrupted his reverie. It fell to his desktop and rolled down, dropping to the floor. A nasty, wetted rolled-up piece of notebook paper. A spitball.

Sully glanced up, annoyed, expecting some smirking classmate, already cottoning to the fact that he was the kind of kid who you could throw spitballs at and not worry about the consequences. He was surprised to see the perpetrator was Tommy, standing outside the classroom and peeking around the edge of the doorframe. Tommy motioned with his finger for Sully to come out. Sully shook his head. Tommy motioned again.

What would Tommy want with him? With some doubt about the wisdom of leaving, but curious, Sully raised his hand. "Mr. Clarence, can I go to the bathroom?"

Mr. Clarence grinned like a jackal, his normal aversion to interruptions overridden by this opportunity. "You mean, may I go to the bathroom?" He ran his tongue over his lower lip, anticipating the squirming misery he was about to witness. Faces perked up around the classroom.

Sully only sighed. "May I go the bathroom?"

Mr. Clarence took a moment before responding,

disappointed at the lack of fun. "Fine, go ahead. Don't dawdle."

Sully paused before getting up and his vision clouded silver for a moment. When it cleared, there stood Mr. Clarence in the same position, wearing the same clothes, only his hair was grayer and he stood in an office. The frosted glass in the door read *Superintendent.* A man behind a desk handed Mr. Clarence a pink slip of paper. His face contorted and glowed red with anger and he shouted something at the man, but the man only shook his head and showed him a newspaper. The headline read *Lawsuit Against School System: Moorestown Teacher Charged.* Mr. Clarence opened his mouth as if to speak again, but instead closed it and abruptly stuffed the paper in his pocket. He exited with shoulders hunched and head down.

And then it passed and Sully was back in the classroom. "Something wrong, Sullahan?" Mr. Clarence asked him. Maybe there was still a chance for fun after all?

"No, nothing," Sully said, and hopped up and out into the hallway. Another of those weird vision things. He shook his head to clear it, hearing Mr. Clarence return to his triangles behind him. At the end of the corridor,

Camo Boy and Tommy waited.

"You seem different lately," Camo Boy said.

"You think so?" Sully said.

"You don't stutter no more," Camo Boy went on. He stuck his forefinger into Sully's chest. "And Dice, she different around you too. Look at you funny. Like she don't hate you."

"And she hate ever'body," Tommy added.

"Is this why you called me out here?" Sully said.

"Nah. You know where Dice is?" Camo Boy asked him. "'Cause she ain't in her classroom."

"I don't know. She disappears a lot." Well, he had a couple ideas where she could be, but he wasn't sharing them with these two. Why did they care where she was, anyway?

A teacher leaned her head out of the nearest classroom door. "Don't you boys have a class you should be in now?"

"Yeah, we was just goin'," Camo Boy said. He nodded at Sully. "Come on, let's go."

Sully didn't want to follow but the teacher was still watching. He trailed Camo Boy down the stairs. "Where are we going? What for?"

"Just keep walkin'," Tommy said, giving him a small

72

shove from behind. "Somebody want to see you."

At the bottom of the stairwell Camo Boy turned into the dusty area behind the stairs and opened a narrow wooden door Sully had never noticed before. *Authorized Personnel Only.* Sully assumed there would be brooms and mop buckets back there, but when he looked in, it was another set of stairs.

"What is this? I'm not going down there," Sully said.

"You got to come," Camo Boy said. "Robo wanna see you."

Robo? What was he doing here? How did he know Camo Boy and Tommy? Didn't he go to a different high school or something? Actually, Sully wasn't sure about that. He tried to read the faces of the two older boys, figure out if they were planning on beating him up or what, but they simply stared back expectantly. He didn't trust them, but he had to know why Robo would be here. Anyway, getting beat up might actually be better than geometry. He descended, and they followed.

# CHAPTER TEN

The stairs were rickety and the room at the bottom was dimly lit by a single uncovered bulb. Boiler tanks and metal shelving stuffed with files, chalkboards on wheels and stacks of moldering textbooks were all jumbled together and reached so far into the gloom Sully couldn't see the end of it. Robo stepped out from behind a rack of band uniforms.

Robo's jaw hung slack, like he'd gotten a shot of novocain at the dentist, and when he spoke, his words came out too slowly. "You did not bring Dice," he said.

"Couldn't find her," Camo Boy said. He gestured to Sully. "And dumbass here didn't know nothin' about her."

"No matter," Robo said. "Maybe we can work with

this."

His speech pattern seemed different too. Different word choices, odd inflections. "Work with what?" Sully asked. "Why are you here?"

"Calm yourself, and all will be clear." Robo closed his eyes and raised his chin.

Camo Boy turned his head and spat a loogie into a dusty corner. "So, we brought the kid, Robo. You got the drum machine here, or we get it later, or what?"

"Patience," Robo said, not opening his lids. "Patience." His face turned rigid and his muscles tensed. He lifted his hands above his head in a stretch and bent his arms behind his head farther than a human's arms should bend.

"Dude," Camo Boy said, wincing. "What the hell are you doing?"

Robo snapped his fingers and a whispering started up in the murky distant shadows of the storage room. Sully recognized the sound right away: his old friends, the weird shadowy shapes.

"Camo Boy, are we gettin' the drum machine?" Tommy said.

The single bulb went out with a buzzing pop.

"Hey, what's goin' on?" Camo Boy shouted.

Sully blinked. He could see perfectly well despite the darkness. All around the edges of the room, the dark shapes glided. They gathered around, creeping up the legs of Camo Boy and Tommy and pulling them to the floor. Robo had fallen to his knees, his torso curving in a bizarre contortion.

Sully glanced up. The door at the top of the stairs was still open a crack. Camo Boy screamed like a little kid and Tommy made little whimpering sounds from where he lay on the ground. Sully was no fan of theirs but he couldn't leave them down here.

Tommy had fallen closest to the stairs. Sully shooed away the shadowy creatures from his body and gave him a shake. A moan, but no other response. He seemed to be asleep. If he was anything like Dice had been under the house, it probably wouldn't be possible to wake him. Sully lifted him by the armpits and dragged him to the stairs.

"Ugh," he said. *Why did I have to start with the chubby one?* He glanced over at Robo and stopped for a moment, horrified but fascinated. Robo was arched completely backwards in a crabwalk position, his stomach exposed, and his abdominal skin splitting open. Blue clawed hands emerged from the rip, grasping at the air. A gurgling came

76

from Robo's throat.

Sully adjusted his grip on Tommy and pulled him up the stairs with redoubled effort. At the top step, Tommy exhaled sharply and sat up as if startled from a dream. "What are you doin'?" he asked, panic in his voice. Robo's gargling had grown louder and higher in pitch and now resembled a wet sort of shriek, and Camo Boy continued to scream.

"It's me."

"Who? Who are you?" Tommy groped blindly with his hands in the darkness.

"Sully. Let's get you out of here."

Sully grabbed one of Tommy's hands and led the older boy up to the door, pushing it open. Tommy stumbled out, Sully a step behind him. Horrible screeches came from the open doorway.

Tommy collapsed to the linoleum floor where he sat with his legs spread in front of him. He stared at Sully with wide eyes and his mouth hanging open. A thought visibly entered his head. "You've got to go back and get Camo Boy," he said.

"No way," Sully said. "I barely got you out. You go back down and get him if you want."

"It's dark down there," Tommy said. "You got some

kind of power. I know you do." The screaming and screeching came to a sudden end and it was quiet. Tommy looked at Sully with frightened eyes and his voice turned plaintive. "Please. We'll give you the watch back. Just go get him. You got to."

"Is that a promise? About the watch?"

"Yeah, I promise. Just go get Camo Boy. Please."

"Fine," Sully said. "Wait for me here. Be ready for when we come up."

# CHAPTER ELEVEN

Sully's conscience fluttered as he descended the stairs again. *I shouldn't have wasted time arguing with Tommy. Of course I can't leave Camo Boy down here, even if he did steal the watch.* Really, he hadn't ever meant to leave him. The truth was he'd stalled because he was scared of what he'd find when he got back down.

At the bottom, Camo Boy was gone. Robo lay in a heap and groaned. His clothes were all torn and his midsection was covered with some kind of foam. Not blood. Sully leaned over and put a finger in it. Sticky, sort of a frothy jelly. But his limbs were normal and his skin was unbroken. Sully had thought he'd be mutilated. Whatever had happened to him, he'd already recovered, mostly.

From somewhere in the back came a chuckle. Sully rose. He was afraid, but also angry, and his anger propelled his feet forward. In the shadow of the boiler and a tangle of pipes, he spotted a movement.

"Who are you?" he shouted as he walked.

"We've met before," came a low, harsh voice. He could briefly make out a figure wearing a fedora, and then it was gone. But he knew who it was: the Blue Man. The one he'd seen outside the school that foggy morning. It'd only been once, but that was enough to ensure he would never forget.

Sully edged past the boiler and found an archway behind it, the echoing sound of footsteps reaching his ears through the opening. He went through and entered a narrow passage. The uneven ground and close walls made it impossible to run, so he settled for fast walking and occasional squeezes when the passage tightened. As he went on, the walls turned from cinderblock to packed soil. The way descended continuously, sometimes by gradual inclinations and other times down steep steps. All the time, the dark shapes swam past on the walls and whispered to him. "Returned, have you? Stay with us this time, perhaps?"

Sully ignored them, intent on the footsteps ahead of him. He almost caught up a couple times, catching sight of the Blue Man as he rounded a corner, carrying over his shoulder a limp body, dressed all in camouflage. But whenever he drew near, the Blue Man took a curve or a twist and disappeared.

Just as he was wondering if the passage would go on forever, Sully reached a closed door. There was no other place the Blue Man could have gone. His heart palpitated and he knew if he hesitated even for a moment he might not have the guts to do it, so he pulled the latch and pushed the door. It opened with a creak.

Beyond lay a huge circular chamber, dim even to Sully's silvery vision, its ceiling so high he could not see it. The Blue Man was nowhere to be seen, but there were doors set in the walls all around, several dozen of them in every direction. It felt to Sully like he'd been here before. Was this the place where he and Dice had been taken when they'd gone underneath the house? That couldn't be right, that place had been earth-hewn. Still, something felt familiar.

No time to dwell on that. He listened for the Blue Man, but the ground was covered in debris, tiles or stones or something, and every time Sully took a step it clattered so loudly he couldn't hear anything above the din. He had no way of knowing which door to choose. He thought he heard something so he stopped and tilted his head. Just barely perceptible, but one noise did come through, a sound that sent a chill through his body. Somewhere, a child was crying.

He debated with himself while the child's distant cries persisted. *I've lost the Blue Man. Maybe I should go back. The way up to the school is still behind me.* But he couldn't leave a little kid crying like that. Then too, maybe the Blue Man was taking Camo Boy to the same place. *Anyway, if I give up now, there's no way I'll ever be able to get back here.*

Sully paced around, kicking aside the trash and stopping periodically to try and pinpoint where the cries originated. He finally seemed to locate the source behind one door, opened just a crack, and he went through. It led to a stone passage that branched repeatedly, and each time he chose the path from which the sound was stronger. Finally he came to a solid wooden door where the crying was much more distinct. Whoever was making the sound was right behind it.

He hesitated, not sure if he should just open the door or what, before deciding on a knock.

"Come in," came a little girl's choked voice.

82

Sully took the latch in his hand and opened the door. He stepped into a large room beyond and was astounded. The floor was carpeted with soft moss, and richly brocaded cloths hung from the walls. There were all sorts of crystals and jewels and things lying about on tables and chests, and vials and bottles full of liquids. Best of all, light and warmth emanated from a fireplace at the far side of the room. Only glowing coals and embers, but true light all the same, not his silvery night vision. He shivered, only now realizing how cold it'd been outside the room.

In the middle of the room stood a little girl, perhaps five, dark-skinned, hair in braids, wearing a purple dress. Oddly, she seemed not quite there, sort of misty, especially around her edges. As if he could almost see through her. She turned to him, her cheeks wet and her eyes puffy.

"I've been waiting for you," she said.

# PART THREE: EURYDICE

# CHAPTER TWELVE

Sully didn't speak for the longest time. Finally, he said, "How did you know I was coming?"

She regarded him with eyes that seemed colder, more appraising, than the eyes of any young child he had ever seen. Maybe it was just a trick of the light from the fireplace flickering across her face, for when she spoke, it was with a little girl's voice, sweet and a little hoarse from crying.

"I heard you outside," she said. "I've been wanting someone to come get me for so long."

"How did you get here?" Sully asked.

"He brought me here. The bad man. He put me in this room and won't let me leave."

"The bad man," Sully said. "You mean the Blue Man?"

"Yes, the blue man," the little girl agreed. "He brought me here and now I can't leave and I want to go home so much."

Sully wasn't sure what to do. One part of him said to take the little girl's hand and run back where he'd come from as fast as possible. He wasn't at all sure he could find his way back, though. But besides that, something seemed off about this whole situation. He wondered if the little girl was telling him the whole truth.

The place smelled of moss and smoke from the fire. He walked slowly around the room, picking up all the little treasures on the various surfaces and handling them, holding jewelry up to inspect, sniffing bottles of perfume, rubbing silk between his finger and thumb. He stopped at a bench covered with old clocks. Cuckoo clocks. Crystal clocks. Tabletop clocks that showed the date or the barometric pressure or the position of various constellations in the sky. Most were in working order but a few lay disassembled, their innards spilling out in a mass of metal and wood.

"Do you mind if I take some of these pieces?" he asked without looking up.

"I don't care," the little girl said.

Sully gathered up parts, whatever looked useful or

interesting, stuffing them in his pockets until they bulged. He pushed one piece of metal aside and gasped at what he found behind it.

His triskelion.

"Where did you get this?" Sully demanded, holding it up.

She shrugged. "I found it. Things end up down here."

He put it in his pocket. The girl regarded him with those un-childlike eyes, tapping her foot with impatience. It made him nervous.

"We've probably wasted enough time," Sully said. "Let's get you out of here."

"A friend of yours is down here," she answered.

Sully knew she meant Camo Boy, although he'd never thought of him as a friend before. "How do you know about that? Do you know where he is?"

"I saw the bad man take him," she said. "He's going to hurt him."

"I want to help him," Sully said. "I want to get both of you out of here. Can you show me where he is?"

The little girl's mouth smiled but those eyes did not. "I can show you."

"Good. Let's go." Sully held out his hand for her to take.

"Oh, but I can't leave yet. Dice has to be here."

A shiver went down Sully's spine. "How do you know who Dice is?"

She was silent for a beat. "The bad man told me. I can't leave unless she's here."

"Why not?" The way this little girl talked made Sully feel like worms were crawling on his skin, and he wasn't sure he believed a word she said.

"It's kind of like a spell." Tears ran down her cheeks. "Please, bring Dice down here, so I can go." A sob shook her frame. "And your friend. When Dice is here, I'll take you to your friend. We'll all go back together. I just want to go home. I've been down here for a really, really long time."

"Okay, okay," Sully said. He hesitantly put his hand on her shoulder. "Don't cry, all right? I'll get Dice."

"You'll come back?" she said, still sobbing. "Please don't leave me here."

"I won't. I promise. I'll be back with Dice as soon as I can." He went to the door. "Do you know how I can get back to school?"

"Ask one of the Shadow Children," she said, her sobs slowing. "They can show you."

"The Shadow Children...those dark shapes?"

90

"Yes, go as fast as you can! Before the bad man comes back!"

Sully didn't have to be told twice. Outside in the corridor, the wooden door swung shut behind him. The shapes swirled around him, but this time he didn't have to force one to show the way.

"Come, come with us," the whispers called, and he followed them around and up, corridor after corridor. Sully recognized nothing of where he'd been before. He wondered who had built this place, and why they'd needed it to be so elaborate. Did it run under the entire town?

The Shadow Children murmured among themselves, but too faintly for him to make out more than a snatch of a phrase here and there. One word he heard repeatedly: queen. "The Queen sent him away, yes," or "Surely the Queen will give rewards, for our work here."

And then he was through a final passage and in bright sunlight, unsure quite where he'd come out from, the whispers retreating behind him. He glanced around and found he stood on the steps in front of the school. The bell rang and within moments students were streaming around him. It was the end of the school day, time to go

91

home. He realized he'd missed his afternoon classes.
Again.

# CHAPTER THIRTEEN

Sully's dad pulled his tie off and tossed it over the back of a chair. He unbuttoned the top two buttons of his shirt, opened the fridge and took out a beer. He fell back into a chair at the kitchen table, sprawling his feet out in front of him.

"Next week should be better," he said, cracking the beer open. "Try an' get home by six. Kids shouldn't have to do the cookin' in the house."

"I don't mind," Sully said, pulling a metal tray out of the oven with an oven mitt. The cheese on the pizza bubbled. He rolled a cutter across it, splattering tomato sauce on the counter. No matter, he'd clean it up later. He loaded two plates with slices and slid one on the table in front of his dad.

His dad went on as if Sully hadn't said anything. "Had

a sale today. Used pickup truck. Not bad. Almost had another one too, but they didn't have no way to qualify for financin'." He took a bite of pizza and continued with the food in one side of his mouth. "What about you? How's your school goin'?"

"Okay, I guess."

"Okay? I ain't gotten any calls since we moved here. I think it must be goin' pretty damn good."

"I guess," Sully said. He felt a prick of guilt. He should tell his dad about all the afternoons he'd missed at school. Not missed, *cut*. He'd get found out eventually anyway. *Three days of math class this week alone,* he thought ruefully. Mr. Clarence had surely noticed his unexcused absences piling up.

"You know what else?" his dad said.

Sully shook his head.

"Your stutter been better lately. I figger you ain't got as much stress." He took a sip of beer. "You know, if my work keeps goin' okay, an' if we see some improvement 'round report card time, maybe I'll get you a cell phone like you been askin' for."

"Maybe," Sully said. If he couldn't even tell his dad about skipping school, how would he explain where his stutter had gone? Not to mention about the voices and the tunnels underneath their house and the school, and the man with blue skin? Sully didn't even know where to begin, so he smiled and ate his pizza. But still, maybe he could start by explaining about the skipping. Better sooner than later.

"Dad? Can I tell you about something?"

But before his dad could answer, there was a knock at the front door. "Who the hell?" he muttered, rising. Sully stopped eating so he could overhear the conversation in the front hall.

"Evenin'," a booming voice said. "I'm Detective Satterfield. This the Kildare residence?"

"Yeah, I'm Jim Kildare," Sully's dad said.

Sully's stomach dropped. A detective. *Because of the shoplifting.* The hardware store must have had a camera or something. But how had they figured out where he lived?

The men talked in the living room while Sully mulled it over. Robo had mentioned they knew him at the hardware store. They must have gotten to him first, and he'd told them about Sully. How could he be so stupid? And he'd felt so proud of himself earlier that week. So brave, stealing paint and running from the store owner. Now he was caught like the thief he was. And the worst thing was he'd have to explain it all to his dad. He fingered the triskelion, pinned again to its usual place on his collar. And it'd brought him the usual luck: bad.

"Sullahan, come in here," his dad said from the other room, his tone grim.

Sully went into the front room with a stomach full of concrete. He wasn't scared, mostly, just sad. A tall man with a blond buzzcut sat on the couch. The detective. Sully was surprised he wasn't in a police uniform, but instead wore a tie and a light blue shirt.

His dad leaned against a stack of boxes, still unpacked. "Detective Satterfield's got a few questions for you, son," his dad said. "You seen the exterminator a couple weeks ago, right?"

"Yes, sir," Sully said. He exhaled in relief. Maybe it wasn't about the shoplifting after all? "Well, I never actually *saw* him."

"I thought you said he was here," his dad said.

"I saw his truck, just not him," Sully said.

"What day did you see his truck?" Detective Satterfield asked.

"Umm, it was two weeks ago or so, after school. Wednesday, I think. And it was still there the next day when I came home from school, too. But it's gone now."

"Huh, wonder where it went to," Detective Satterfield

said. He wrote a note in a small notebook and looked up at Sully. "But you never saw the man?"

"No. He's been missing, hasn't he?" Sully asked.

"That's right," the detective said, leaning forward. "How do you know that?"

On a whim, Sully decided he liked the detective. His cologne smelled nice and he seemed understanding. Even when he asked hard questions there was something gentle in his manner. "I found his hat. Do you want to see it?"

Detective Satterfield's eyebrows lifted. "Oh, I'll definitely want to take a look at that." He jotted another note down.

Sully ran up to his room and came back down with the cap. His initial relief that the visit wasn't about the shoplifting had faded. Before, the voices and tunnels had all seemed like a thing between him and Dice and the others, scary but somehow not quite believable. Now that adults were involved, he knew the situation was real, and couldn't be ignored. After losing Camo Boy, he had a bad feeling about what fate might have befallen the exterminator.

He handed the hat over, and Detective Satterfield examined it, running his finger around the brim and the interior. He looked up at Sully. "Where'd you find this?"

"In the crawlspace."

"Let's go look." The adults rose and Sully led them to the backyard, around to the exact spot behind the boxwoods. It was dark out and an overcast night, so Sully thought at first that was the reason he couldn't see the door. But when the detective turned on a flashlight and illuminated the spot, there was only plain brick around the bottom of the house.

Sully ran his fingers over the rough surface. "I could've sworn the door was here," he said. "It was iron, with all kinds of things in the metal. Like pictures and things."

Sully's dad shook his head. "What're you talking about, boy? I thought the crawlspace was on the other side." And sure enough when they went to see, on the front of the house behind a rose bush was a plain square wooden door, clearly visible in the flashlight beam.

"Is this where you found the hat?" Detective Satterfield asked. He dropped to his knees and opened the door, peering in.

"Yeah, this must be it," his dad said. "You were just confused, weren't you, Sullahan?"

"I... I..." Yet another thing he couldn't explain. "Yeah, I guess I must have been." It was a lie, but he'd look pretty stupid insisting there'd been another door.

"Well, I don't spot anything unusual under there," Detective Satterfield said, standing up again. He gave Sully's dad a business card. "Thanks for your help, Mr. Kildare. Do you mind if I come around tomorrow and take a more thorough look under the house?"

"Be my guest," Sully's dad said.

"And if you have any other information that might be helpful, please give me a call. And that goes for you too, son," Detective Satterfield said. He handed Sully a card as well, and shook both their hands. "Y'all have a good evenin'." At the street he opened the door of a nondescript sedan and drove off.

Sully continued staring at the wooden door underneath the house. He guessed that if he opened it up and went in, it would lead nowhere but under the floorboards.

# CHAPTER FOURTEEN

Sully sat at his desk, integrating the parts he'd found in the little girl's room into the carriage clock. He'd awakened early and wanted to see if he could have it running before school, but mainly he tinkered to calm his mind. His conversation with the little girl still troubled him, and somehow he knew when he got back to school the wooden doorway down to the basement would be gone, just like the crawlspace. So how was he supposed to get Dice down there? And would he even want to, if he could? Of course, if another doorway did show up, the real difficulty would be getting her to accompany him. She wasn't exactly easy to convince if something wasn't her idea. Besides all that, he had to warn her about Robo, and his connection with the Blue Man. He'd have to broach the topics with her delicately.

Adding the new parts to the clock was easy, once he figured out the way they fit, clicking together or sliding over the existing pieces. Almost too easy, really, and once or twice he had the vague impression the parts were changing their size or shape when he turned his head. But of course that wasn't possible. He must have misjudged them in the first place.

Odd, though, the innards were so strange-looking now, with gears and joints sticking out unnaturally, and when he wound it up and things started moving, it looked as if it were breathing, expanding in and out. Nor did the hands tick regularly. Rather, they remained perfectly still for two or three minutes and then advanced with a sudden jerk. He wasn't really sure why, and no amount of adjusting seemed to make a difference.

Still, it did keep time correctly, and once he put the casing over the mechanism, it looked fine too. Maybe he should return it to Mr. Brown today. He decided against it. He wanted to try to coax the hands into moving more smoothly, and then he'd bring it back.

"Sullahan, come down for breakfast," came his father's bellowing voice. It was late in the fall now and the sun was not yet up though it was past seven.

"Yes, sir," Sully yelled back. He put the clock down on

his desk, picked up his backpack, and went down to eat. Had he remained behind, he would have seen a movement on the face of the clock, a little oval opening up that looked almost like an eye.

---

Sully and Dice breached the gap in the chain-link fence, holding the sharp edges of the fence fabric back with their hands and squeezing through. *Yet another day of skipping school*, Sully reflected with regret. But Dice had said she had something to show him and she didn't want Robo to know about it. He couldn't pass this opportunity up.

On the other side of the fence, a covered rail shed was packed full of train cars waiting to be coupled or shifted. Weeds grew up in the gravel between the rails and an electrical buzzing came from a building in the corner with a sign reading *Machine Shop*.

"Shouldn't there be some workers around or something?" Sully asked.

"There never are," Dice said. "Come on, let's take a look."

She led him between a pair of green hopper cars. Sully noticed their sides were covered with the intricate graffiti letters known as wildstyle, their overlapping lines so convoluted it was nearly impossible for an amateur to make out. In fact, nearly every car in the yard was tagged. Somebody'd really bombed this place. He smiled at himself. A couple weeks ago those words would have been gibberish and now he was using them like a real writer, even if it was only in his head. It was like a secret language known only to initiates.

"Up there," Dice said, pointing to a panel in the corrugated metal roof, right over a reflective silver chemical tanker car.

"How will we get up there?" Sully asked.

Just then voices came from the direction of the machine shop. Two men, maybe more.

"I thought there were never any workers around," Sully whispered to her.

"Come on," Dice whispered back. She darted to the side of the tanker car and put her hand on the bottom rung of a ladder welded to the middle of its body.

"Is it safe?" Sully asked before she could start up.

Dice rolled her eyes. "Just keep quiet. And follow me."

She climbed the ladder, easily maneuvering onto the top of the tanker car. She straddled the silvery rounded body and pushed herself forward. The voices grew louder and Sully hurried up after her, swinging one leg over at the top onto the cool silvery tank. There were some fittings and a pressure release valve at the top but he scooted over them and followed Dice.

Two men came around the corner of a box car. They wore white hard hats and gray work overalls, and one carried a clipboard. Dice and Sully pressed themselves flat against the metal. It was pretty dark, but if the men looked up, they would still be clearly visible. Sully closed his eyes. Why did he let Dice talk him into these situations?

They men didn't look up. They kept walking, their voices faded, and Dice resumed her inching along. Sully opened his eyes. When they reached the place where they were underneath the panel in the roof, she sat up and said, "Hold my feet."

Sully gripped her ankles and she stood with her arms out for balance, ducking so her head wouldn't bump against the metal. The panel had two long sliding bolts holding it against the building frame. One opened easily, but the other wouldn't budge. She hammered against it with her palm. Sully was sure at any moment she would lose her balance and slip down the rounded side, but she was steady and after several palm strikes the bolt unlodged.

She gave the panel a shove and it flew open on its hinges, flipping back onto the roof with a thud that reverberated across the whole shed and opened a dazzling portal of daylight, a beacon in the roof.

"Shit," Dice said under her breath. She put her hands over the edges. "Give me a boost."

Sully lifted her feet while she scrambled up. He pulled himself up after her and closed the panel, expecting the whole while for the men to come back.

The top of the roof was glaring white and chilled with a fierce wind that set Sully's eyes to watering. A steel latticework held an industrial tank positioned directly over them. A hatch on its bottom opened over the roof panel, presumably to pour its contents into waiting railcars below.

"They'll be here any minute, you know." Sully yelled to be heard above the wind.

"They won't have any idea where we went," Dice yelled back.

She strolled out to the center of the roof and gazed up at the tank, a thick cylinder rising thirty feet in the air. Except for an access ladder it was unadorned, a huge expanse of white-painted metal. Sully leaned close to her, as much to shelter himself from the wind as to talk.

"There it is," she said, leaning her head to his ear so as to only have to raise her voice slightly. "My heaven spot. And look over there." She pointed to the arch of the highway bridge rising up from its moorings on the banks of the Newstead River only a couple hundred yards away, its deck almost even with the roof of the train shed. Semis roared across the blue-gray expanse, their tires whooshing loud over the concrete and metal-gridded road surface. "Everybody who drives over that bridge'll see it. Thousands of people every day, checking out my piece."

"How're you going to write?" Sully asked. "You can't hold onto the ladder with one hand and paint with the other."

"Duh. How else?" Dice said.

Sully shook his head. "Looks precarious. And what if the cops catch you up here?"

"So what if they do?"

"Aren't you afraid of going to jail?"

"Nope." She sat down facing the tank and took her backpack off.

Sully sat beside her. The cold of the metal roof chilled him through the seat of his pants and he shivered, wrapping his arms around his body. "I don't get something. Why are you involved in all this graffiti stuff, anyway?"

Dice gave him a withering look. "I want people to see me. To know *my* name."

"Why? Do you want to be rich?"

"I don't care about money," she said. "I just want people to know who I am. That I spent time on this earth." She pulled her black book out and folded it open to a blank page, seemingly impervious to the temperature. "Just like everybody wants."

"Not me."

Dice pulled out a pencil and sketched, outlining the tank and marking the page with arrows and measurements. Sully wasn't sure she'd heard him, but then she leaned over and spoke in his ear. "Well I do. Someday, when they all know my name, they won't be able to ignore me."

"I don't ignore you," Sully said.

Dice went back to sketching but continued talking, maybe more to herself than to him. He strained to hear her words. "After I put up my piece, people gonna remember me then. A hundred years from now, they'll look at this heaven spot with tears in their eyes. Like the Mona Lisa. Generations of people, they'll say, 'Who was it put that there?' And they'll see my tag and know who it was: Dice. That black girl nobody ever gave two shits about. All them other famous people, they'll be dead and gone. But my name will still be on everybody's lips."

Her words drifted off while she traced letters and figures. The wind died down for a moment and there was a lull in the bridge traffic, creating an unexpected quiet.

"Don't tell Robo about this, you know," she said.

"Why not?"

"If he knew about up here he'd have it covered with paint in a heartbeat."

Sully nodded. It seemed a good time to warn her about the Blue Man and his connection with Robo, tell her about the disappearing doors underneath the house and in the basement of the school, explain how she had to go with him to save the little girl and Camo Boy. "I went back again, to that place we went under my house," he said.

"Did you now?"

"Yeah, and you need to come back down there too. There's this little girl and—"

"I ain't never going back down there," Dice said, without looking up.

Sully stopped. This tactic wasn't working. He'd try

another. "Robo's dangerous, you know."

"He wouldn't hurt nobody."

"Well, maybe he wouldn't normally, but he's not himself." Dice's expression turned sour but Sully kept going. He had to let her know. "When we were under my house, I think we let something out. And it's sort of…taken control of Robo."

The wind picked up and Dice raised her voice to be heard. "Sullahan, that is the most pitiful excuse I've ever heard."

"It's not an excuse! It's this man…this thing, he's really dangerous, and he took Camo Boy away." Even as he said it he knew how weak it must sound to her ears.

"Look, I don't wanna hear no more about it." Dice stood, and her voice had an edge of anger. "It was a mistake bringing you up here. If you're jealous of Robo, just keep your opinion to yourself."

"Jealous! What would I be jealous of?"

She walked over to the panel and pulled it open, put her feet over the edge.

*Oh, God*, Sully thought to himself. *She's leaving. She thinks it's some kind of romance thing. That I like her and I'm jealous of Robo. Could I have said it any worse?* "Wait, Dice, give me a chance," he called out. "Let me just explain it."

She held her hand up to stop him. "Don't bother. And don't sit with me tomorrow, either." She lowered herself down and disappeared from view.

He fingered the triskelion on his collar. *More bad luck. How in hell am I going to rescue Camo Boy now?* And then another thought popped in his head. *Do I like her? Like that?*

A sheet of yellow paper flew across the roof, whipped by the cold north wind that cut right through Sully's jacket. It caught against his leg for a moment, and Sully reached down with a benumbed hand to grab it. He was about to let it fly away but on a whim he stuffed it in his pocket instead.

# CHAPTER FIFTEEN

"Spot me, all right?" Tommy said as he laid back on the weight bench. He lifted the barbell from its position on the rack and lowered it to his chest, then raised it with a ferocious grunt.

Sully looked on, bored. The lifting session had gone on forty-five minutes and Tommy showed no signs of flagging. *How did I get myself into this?* Tommy'd found him between classes poking around under the stairwell where the wooden door had been. As Sully had expected, it'd been gone, just like the door to the crawlspace.

For the rest of the day, Tommy had been attached to Sully like a lamprey. At least eating together at lunch had given him a place to sit—"Don't even think about it," Dice had said when he'd neared her table with his tray. But the between-class fist bumps, the offer to share a cigarette in a stall in the boy's bathroom, the walk home side by side? Way too much. He'd regretted it as soon as he'd admitted in Tommy's driveway he didn't have any plans for the afternoon. And now here he was.

"Dude, you wanna break in here?" Tommy said.

"What?" Sully's head snapped up, his reverie broken.

"You wanna lift for a minute? I gotta rest between sets."

"No, that's all right," Sully said.

"'Kay," Tommy said and squirted water into his mouth from a large green water bottle before lying back on the bench again.

Sully shivered and pulled his jacket tight around him while Tommy lifted. He had no idea how Tommy could stand it with only a t-shirt on. The garage wasn't heated, nor did its cinderblock walls provide sufficient insulation against the chilly November day outside. He put his hands in his jacket pocket. *Why is there crumpled up paper in there?* He pulled it out. The yellow paper from when he'd been on top of train shed. It looked like a flyer of some sort. He pressed it against the wall and smoothed out the wrinkles:

*Underground Rave Party!!!*
*With Surprise DJ*

The letters were puffy and connected together, almost like a well-done graffiti tag. Around the paper's edges, a lot of intricately lined pictures formed a frame around the message. Something about them caught his eye.

"What's that?" Tommy said, peering over his shoulder.

"Nothing important," Sully said. He put his head closer, trying to figure out what the pictures around the edges were.

Tommy reached out and grabbed it, looked it over. "Resurrection Baptist? That's that old abandoned church downtown. Me and Camo Boy go in there to smoke sometimes. When's November 16ᵗʰ?"

"This Friday," Sully said. His ears had perked up at the mention of an abandoned church. Was it the same one he'd been in?

"Cool! I'm goin'," Tommy said, handing the flyer back and selecting a dumbbell from a rack against the wall. "What about you? We could go together."

"I don't know. I really need to look for another way to go get Camo Boy. You saw the door wasn't there anymore."

"Yeah, that was weird," Tommy said. "I'll help you look for a new door. Tomorrow, we'll do it? Right?"

"Maybe not. It might be something I have to do on my own," Sully said.

"Alone, right." Tommy dropped a dumbbell on the floor with a ringing clank. "It's the watch, ain't it?"

"What?"

"The watch we took. You're still sore about it."

"It's not the watch," Sully said. Well, it was, at least partly. And now that Camo Boy was gone, he was supposed to be best friends with Tommy all of a sudden? Anyway, even if the watch incident had never taken place, he didn't want Tommy sticking to him while he figured things out.

"Right. Look, Camo Boy has it. He'll give it to you when he comes back. I'll tell him to."

"Okay. Thanks. But you know, I don't know if the doors open for just anybody," Sully said, trying to get off the subject. "I think it'll work better if it's only me."

"Yeah, if you say so," Tommy said, lying back on the bench and positioning himself under the bar. "You're the one who got the powers."

Sully put the flyer back in his pocket and zipped his jacket all the way to the top.

114

"You cold?" Tommy asked him, his head turned horizontally towards Sully.

"Yeah, it's freezing in here."

"If you're cold, it means you ain't workin' out enough." He performed half a dozen reps and slid the barbell back on the rack. "My brother used to tell me that, before he had to leave."

"Where'd he go?" Sully asked.

"Prison," Tommy said. He paused, but Sully didn't say anything so he went on. "For stealin' a car. Five years. And you know what?"

"What?"

"The day after he went in, that was the exact day me and Camo Boy met each other."

"Huh," Sully said, not sure what else to say. "I think I have to go home now."

"No, wait!" Tommy said, sitting up straight. "You want a snack? Somethin' to eat?"

Sully had already watched Tommy eat a leftover Tupperware of Hamburger Helper and a bag of potato chips. He shook his head.

"We could head down to Jerry's," Tommy said. Sully looked at him blankly. "Jerry's Bait Shop. He don't card if you buy cigarettes. Me and Camo Boy done it plenty of times." He picked up a pair of dumbbells and cranked out some arm curls.

"No, I should really get home and cook dinner before my dad arrives," Sully said. "He gets mad if I don't have dinner ready."

"Oh," Tommy said. "I guess that makes sense." He put down the dumbbells and hit the button on the garage door opener. The door rumbled up, vibrating the concrete floor and rattling the metal weight plates. "But I can help you, if you need somethin'. Findin' a new door, whatever. Let me know."

"Yeah, I'll do that." Sully exited into the bitter cold evening. The sun was already setting. "If I think of something," he called back.

His teeth were soon chattering uncontrollably but despite that, Sully stopped under a street lamp and pulled the flyer out again. Something was bothering him. He inspected the pictures around the edges closely. Big, tentacled creatures with mechanical faces and wires and tubes sticking out. It reminded him a lot of the sketches he'd seen in Robo's black book. The abandoned church, the familiar pictures. It seemed like there were a lot of connecting parts here, even if he couldn't piece them together yet. He remembered the fire from his vision in the church. This whole situation gave him a bad feeling. He decided that even if he didn't go with Tommy, he definitely needed to pay a visit to the party.

———————

To his surprise, the lights were already on at his house. He opened the front door, grateful to get into the warm air. He could tell right away his dad's early return was bad news. Didn't even have to see him. The clink of a beer can on the kitchen table explained it all. Sully stood for long moments without moving. A burden heavier than Tommy's barbells weighed on him.

After a long while, his dad called out, "You home, boy?"

"Yeah, Dad. I'm home." He wondered what this early arrival was due to. He had the fleeting thought his teacher had called his dad at work about his skipping school. But that wouldn't bring him home early. And anyway, if that'd been it, his dad would already be yelling. No, this was something else, something worse.

He entered the kitchen with dread pooling in his stomach. "Should I get dinner started, Dad?"

His dad shook his head. "Ain't hungry. Make somethin' if you want it." He took a long slug from his beer can. "Bring me another of these, when you got a sec."

There were already two empties on the table. Sully hesitated, decided to go ahead with what he had to say. "Are you sure you need another one?"

"Just bring me a goddamn beer, boy. I don't need a lecture from no kid."

Stupid. He'd approached it all wrong, his words too obvious. Like with Dice on top of the train shed. Even without the stutter, words never seemed to work for him. Sully retrieved another can from the refrigerator and put it down in front of his dad. "Is everything all right?"

"No, everything ain't all right." Silence. And after a minute, nobody moving, Sully barely even breathing, his Dad spoke again. "Slam dunk sale and I didn't make it."

Sully groped for the right thing to say. He knew his Dad needed something, some comfort, some encouragement. But there was about as much chance of Sully coming up with the right words as finding a million dollars in his sock drawer.

"Long-time customers," his dad continued. "Always bought from the dealership for years and years. Manager gave it to me as a gimme. But I guess they didn't want to buy a car from some redneck dressed up in a suit." He cracked open the beer and drained half of it in one pull.

As Sully stared, he felt the heat of the silver start at the top of his eyes. He screwed his lids shut, tried to force the silver back. Not now. He couldn't stand it now; whatever vision was coming, he didn't want it. The silver was gaining, but he fought it, willed it back wherever it came from. And when he opened his eyes again, it was gone. His dad still sat with his expression of guilty bafflement, like somebody who knows he's done wrong but isn't sure how he got into it.

Sully breathed in deeply. "Dad, will we have to move again?"

"I don't know," his dad said softly.

Sully thought about making something for himself. Macaroni and cheese, maybe. But he realized he wasn't too hungry either. He thought he'd work on his clock a while. "I'm going up to my room now."

His dad responded with a slight nod but didn't speak.

---

Sully lay in his bed and stared at the ceiling. He'd already helped his dad to bed, pulled off his shoes, put a blanket over him. It'd been easy to clean up the kitchen. Just throw away all the empty cans, make sure the lights were turned off. But sleeping, that was hard. He had the strangest feeling somebody was watching him, although he had the shade pulled down over the window. He tried to remember if he'd had a decent night's sleep since they'd moved to Moorestown, but couldn't recall one.

It was probably past midnight when he finally drifted off into slumber. It was then the whispers came from within the walls. His eyes snapped open and he glared with anger, not that they could see him from behind the drywall. "Go away!" he shouted. "I know you're just children!"

But the whispers didn't stop. They grew louder and more distinct. "What has he seen?" they said. "Enjoyed the gift? Yes, yes, the Sight? Seen things he won't forget? Secrets? Hidden thoughts? Visions of things yet to come?"

"I've seen things," Sully admitted. He sat up in bed and put his feet over the side. Obviously he wasn't going to be getting any sleep. "But they haven't scared me, if that's what you think."

The whispers laughed. "Not scared! Does he want to know what we see? When we look at him? Does he want to know what he looks like to us?"

"Fine," Sully sighed. "Tell me what I look like to you."

More laughing, giggling even, as if the voices were delighted with the prospect of telling him. "Yes, yes, we see him. In a dark place, deep and forgotten. He, and his friends too, and others. Many others. All forgotten, yes, even to those who once loved him. Bones picked clean. And the Hunger, gnawing on him. Perhaps a rib bone, yes?"

"The Hunger?" Sully said. "Is that…the Blue Man?"

"The blue one, yes, the Hunger," the voices agreed. "Gnawing the bones. But that's not his favorite part. Not the tastiest morsel, no, no. His favorite part, he dips his fingers in it and licks them clean, better than fat, better than marrow. He chews it for a long time, weeks and weeks, lets the succulent juices drip down his throat and moans with the taste of it."

Sully barely dared to ask, but could not resist. "What is his favorite part?" he said in a whisper.

More giggling. "The soul, of course, the soul! Yes, yes, he chews and chews and moans and moans. Very painful! Agony for weeks and months. We remember well."

Now Sully truly did shiver. But if he was afraid, he was also angered. He beat his fist against the wall and shouted. "How dare you come in my house! Nobody asked you to come here and interrupt my sleep!"

The voices fled from his pounding and didn't return, not that night. Not until the evening at the church did he see them again. But the damage was done: when the dawn came, he still sat on the edge of his bed, feet dangling down, not having slept a bit.

# CHAPTER SIXTEEN

Sully stared in amazement as Tommy inserted an entire Salisbury steak into his mouth and proceeded to chew it like a hyena at the kill. Gravy ran down his chin and dripped onto his black t-shirt. And Sully had thought his lunchtimes couldn't get any worse. He watched, disgusted yet fascinated, until he couldn't bear it anymore and had to turn his head.

"Why do you have to eat like that?" he asked.

"'Cause I'm hungry," Tommy replied around a mouthful of food. "You gonna eat that?" He gestured at Sully's untouched plate.

Sully pushed his tray over and leaned back in his chair.

Naturally his eye sought Dice, finding her alone at her usual table. But once spotting her, he had to check twice. She was dressed in black from head to toe: black shoes, black skirt, black blouse, even black hat and gloves. She looked like a woman in mourning in one of those old black-and-white movies, far too formal for a school day. All she was missing was a veil. She seemed to be singing to herself, but glanced up when she sensed him looking at her. Sully quickly turned his head back to Tommy, who was jamming a cinnamon roll between his lips.

"Hey, you find anything out about Camo Boy yet?"

"I don't know," Sully said. He was pretty sure Tommy was going to ask him that question every day until he had an answer. "I'm really trying to figure out a way to get back to that place. It's taking a lot of my time."

This was true. He'd been racking his brain, trying to remember everything about his previous visits to that strange underground world, hoping some detail would provide a clue to locating another door. Randomly opening janitor closets around the school was getting him nothing but strange looks from other kids. But since he was having no luck with that conundrum, he decided to turn his attention to the possibly more solvable mystery of Dice's unusual choice in outfits.

In the hallway between classes Sully caught up with Dice at her locker. He stood behind her for a minute, a couple feet back. He cleared his throat. No response. He knew she knew he was there but she ignored him completely, so he stepped right beside her, pushing himself into her personal space. "Okay, why are you wearing all black?" he asked.

"'Cause today's my birthday," she said without making eye contact.

Sully sighed. "Why do you have to be so weird? Just tell me the truth."

She dropped a book in her bag and slammed the locker door closed. "You know, I liked you better when you had a stutter."

Sully was about to reply, but bit his lip. "Fine," he said, finally. "Happy birthday."

She strode off without answering.

The rest of the afternoon, an idea formulated itself in Sully's mind: he'd follow Dice home, or wherever she went after school. After all, the time he'd followed her before, he'd found out about the graffiti. He was pretty sure she wouldn't go out tagging this time, not dressed like that. But maybe wherever she went would prove as interesting.

As soon as the bell rang he bulleted out the classroom door, through the hallway, down the steps, and through the front gate. He waited behind the wooden pole of a streetlight, watching the stream of kids passing by on the sidewalk. He was a little nervous she wouldn't go the front way like a normal person. *Who knows, maybe she climbs the fence every day? Crawls through a tunnel? Hitches a ride on a garbage truck? You can't tell with that girl.* No, there she was, still in all black, walking alone with her head held up.

He maintained a discreet distance to keep her from seeing him, but she never looked back. Her pace was slow, almost a funeral march, but she didn't deviate, didn't stop to talk to any trees or pet friendly dogs or pick flowers, just went straight home. In fact, Sully had never seen her so intent. At her house, he watched from the corner. She stood outside the door for several minutes, standing quietly. She lifted the latch and went in.

Once she was inside, he hid himself behind a shrubbery in front of her house. A long time passed, maybe twenty minutes. He hadn't counted on that. *Maybe she's not doing anything or going anywhere. Maybe she simply dresses in black on her birthday.* It struck him his plan hadn't really been that well thought out and he might end up sitting here an awful long time.

At that moment, the front door opened again and Dice walked out with her parents. He could see their legs descending the stairs, her mother in heels, her father in wingtips. His shoes were shined and the dark pants crisply pressed. Maybe they were headed to church?

The three sets of legs reached the sidewalk and stopped. The wingtips spun around. They were approaching his hiding place. Sully tried to use the power of his mind to open a hole in the ground to sink into, but no good. He looked up hesitantly to find Dice's dad, wearing an irritated expression.

"Son, what do you think you're doing in our yard?"

"I… I…" Not stuttering, only a lack of a good response. *What* am *I doing in their yard?*

"He followed me home," Dice said. "I don't know why."

"I wanted to see why Dice was so dressed up," Sully said. He should have lied, he thought, because the truth sounded pretty stupid.

"Why didn't you ask her?" her dad asked.

"I did," Sully said. "She's not talking to me right now."

"Dad, just let him come, okay?" came Dice's voice.

Her dad looked him up and down. Sully was clearly underdressed for whatever occasion they were going to attend. He thought her dad would probably turn around and walk off. But after a moment he said, "Well, come on

127

then. Dice, open the door for him."

Sully stood. Dice stood by a black Lexus, polished and gleaming. He climbed in the door Dice held open for him. The interior was all white leather and smelled like her mom's perfume, musk and jasmine and vanilla. A lot different than his dad's pickup truck and its floorboards strewn with fast-food wrappers. The seatbelt automatically wrapped around him when he closed the door.

Dice and her parents got in without a word. Her dad put the car in drive and gently pressed the accelerator. Sully wondered if he would ask him about the broken clock, but he didn't say a word, and neither did anybody else. Dice's mom held her head up and stared straight ahead, her face as rigid and controlled as a poker player's. Dice herself looked out her window and pretended like nobody else was there. Sully didn't dare break the silence.

A light rain fell, misting the windshield. The squeak of the wipers against the glass was the only sound. They drove through Moorestown's shabby little downtown and headed north along a narrow, two-lane highway into the piney woods. At a little wooden church with peeling paint, her dad pulled into the gravel lot. *Emmanuel Methodist Episcopal Church*, the sign read.

Behind the church was a cemetery on a small hill. They got out and went through the gate. No trees, only patchy grass and weeds. There were a few dozen graves, most marked by simple flat stones. A little path led to a mausoleum, a huge marble edifice surrounded by a wrought-iron fence, separate from and far more elaborate than the rest of the graveyard. That's the place they approached.

The mausoleum had a sort of window in its side, but instead of glass it held a ceramic plaque. Underneath some writing in Latin, a bas-relief sculpture showed an angel blessing a woman who had fallen on her back. A few feet from the mausoleum was a headstone topped with a cross. Dice's parents stood next to each other in front of it, Dice a few feet back. She gazed at the overcast sky, the trees, her hands, anywhere but the grave. It was raining harder now, the red clay dirt turning muddy under their shoes. Dice's mom opened an umbrella. She'd brought a single white rose with her and she bent down and gently placed it in front of the headstone. In the distance a truck went by on the highway, its tires loud on the wet pavement.

Sully took a step closer so he could read the words of the inscription. It read:

Eurydice Ella Brown

Born June 5th, 2000

Died November 12th, 2005

*The day we will never forget,*

*when from our home you strayed.*

*Our hearts will ever long,*

*our love will never fade.*

Sully read the words over, and a third time. The name, the dates. It made no sense.

"But!" he said out loud, and the others turned their heads sharply. "But that's Dice's name!"

# CHAPTER SEVENTEEN

His words hung in the air, the faces of Dice's parents shocked at the intrusion. "Have some respect!" her mother hissed. "This is a sacred place."

"Mom, give him a break," Dice said. "He don't know."

"He *doesn't* know. How many times have I told you about using that hoodlum talk, young lady?" She gripped the umbrella handle so hard veins were popping out on her hands.

Sully shuddered and there was another of those silver washes across his eyes. Everything was dark for a second and when he could see again, things were changed. It was no longer raining, but the trees were bare and the air bitter cold. Patches of snow dotted the unmowed grass and covered the path from the hill down to the mausoleum. Dice and her dad were gone, but her mom was still there. She appeared younger, her face smoother, her hair without any flecks of gray. The headstone, too, was new, a layer of snow around its base stark white against the polished dark marble.

She knelt before the headstone, and Sully watched her weep. When she rose Sully noticed a round belly bulging out from under her shirt. She was pregnant, and almost due, judging from her size. She dabbed a tissue at her eyes and turned to go, but before she could take a step her face distorted in an expression of pain. She put a hand on the headstone to steady herself. Sully tried to go to her, do something to help her, but he couldn't move. *Of course not. This is a vision, it's not happening now.*

She held herself for a minute before recovering. Sully wondered if that's what a contraction looked like. *This must be the day Dice was born. Even on the day she gave birth to Dice, she visited this cemetery.* And then everything went dark and when Sully opened his eyes again he was back with Dice and her parents in the rain.

"Dice, is there something wrong with this boy?" her mother said.

Sully realized his knees must have buckled during his vision. Although he hadn't fallen, his body swayed crazily on unsteady legs. He pulled himself up straight.

"I'm fine," he said. "I felt a little, umm, dizzy for a second."

"Dice, take your friend and go on a walk, okay?" Dice's dad said. "Your mother and I would like some quiet."

Dice's eyes were hot with anger, but she obeyed. She went out the gate and into the grassy strip along the highway, Sully behind her. She led them behind the church and onto a little path leading into the woods. It was dryer under the trees and the rhythmic pattering of raindrops in the branches of the loblollies above them sounded a jagged static in their ears.

They hiked a quarter hour or more with hair dripping and no words between them, winding along wherever the path followed. It was Sully who spoke first. "Dice?"

"I know what you're going to say, so don't even bother."

So Sully didn't. He waited until Dice was ready to speak again, and in a little while, she was.

"You know, when I was little, I never even knew about birthdays," she said. "It wasn't until I got to school and heard everybody else talkin' about birthday party this and birthday present that. That's when I figured it out."

"So you didn't know what day you were born?" Sully asked.

"Don't be stupid. Of course I knew. We came here every year. And that's the day I turned one year older."

"So you never had a party?"

"Never." They had reached a little wooden footbridge. It was arched over a creek, its waters swollen and swift from the wet weather. They stopped on the wooden planks and looked out at the roiling rush below them. Dice turned to him. "She was my sister."

"But she died—"

"Died before I was born. Yeah. One year exactly."

"And your parents gave both of you the same name?" Sully said, not quite sure he had it straight. Although he was pretty sure getting it straight wouldn't help it make any more sense.

"Yeah, the exact same name," Dice said. "And I don't want to talk about it anymore."

"Can I say one more thing?"

"What?" Dice's voice had an irritated edge.

"Happy birthday."

Dice froze, and tears welled up in her eyes.

"What's wrong?" Sully asked.

"No one's ever done that before."

Sully shook his head in confusion. "Ever done what?"

"No one's ever told me 'Happy Birthday.' And you've done it twice in one day." And Dice cried right there on the bridge, the water dripping from her cheeks into the splashing creek below. Sully didn't really know what to do, but he felt he couldn't just stand there, so he put his arms around her. She didn't push him away.

"You know something else?" Sully said when Dice had calmed down a bit. "You don't have the same name as her."

She gave him a confused glance.

"Her name was Eurydice, but yours is Dice. It's not the same."

She stared at him, her face close to his. He wondered if they were about to kiss. Their lips neared. And then he heard the cry of a little girl over the sound of the creek.

"Do you hear that?" he asked, snapping his head back.

"Yeah, sounds like a little kid."

Sully had a good idea who it was. They ran down the far side of the bridge and followed the noise across a muddy field, their feet sloshing in the mucky earth. The cry came from the far side of the field, in a little stand of juniper. They pushed through the dark, scratchy branches and found a natural stone grotto in a little open circle.

The crying clearly emanated from the rocky opening. Sully and Dice looked at each other.

"Can I ask you a question?" Sully said.

"Right now? Somebody's in trouble in there."

She made a move to go in, but Sully grabbed her elbow. "This'll be fast. How did your sister die?"

Dice gave him a look to let him know he was breaking one of her rules, but she answered anyway. "Nobody knows. She disappeared one day."

"But her body, what happened to it?"

"Goddamn it, Sully!"

Sully tightened his grip. He hoped this wouldn't lead to the silent treatment again but he had to know. "What happened to her body?"

She glared at him. "Her body was never found, all right? Somebody took her and she disappeared. That's all I know."

Sully let go and nodded. His suspicion was confirmed. No body. Dice's sister had never really died. The little girl he'd met under the school must be her. She had said she could leave when he brought Dice with him. Well, he had Dice now and this was clearly an entrance. He could bring back the girl, and Camo Boy too. He'd even ask if she knew about the exterminator. *This is it. It's all about to work out. So why am I afraid?*

He stuffed the fear down, something he was getting good at. "Let's go in," he said.

# PART FOUR:
# THE HUNGER

# CHAPTER EIGHTEEN

Sully emerged from the trees holding the little girl's hand. Blood trickled bright red from his nose and spread rusty brown across the shredded knee of his pants. One cheek throbbed purple with bruising. Mud covered his clothes. The little girl was dirty, too, but she wore a purple dress and her eyes were triumphant.

At the cemetery the rain had stopped and a break in the clouds let sunlight filter down onto the graves. He led the girl around the chain-link fence. Dice's mother was still at the headstone, on her knees with her eyes closed and her hands holding the side of the stone. Her dad stood off to the side, lost in thought.

"Mama?" the little girl said as they entered the gate.

Dice's mom looked over her shoulder. Her eyes widened, her mouth fell open. Dice's dad looked too, and simply froze when he spotted the girl, paused like one of the broken watches Sully liked to fix. For a second, Sully wasn't sure bringing the little girl back was a good idea.

"Mama? Daddy? Did you miss me?"

And then Dice's mom was on her feet and had the girl in her arms in an instant, holding her tight, not letting go. "Eurydice? Is that you? Oh my God, Eurydice!" Black mascara rivulets ran from her eyes over her cheeks. "You came back to us. I always knew you would!"

Dice's dad was there, too, his hand on his wife's back, the other on his daughter's head, murmuring her name while he stroked her hair, her cheek, the flowing purple dress. He turned and noticed Sully. He looked unsure when he saw Sully's wounds and his stricken face. Maybe he took the boy's expression for an accusation. "We've been looking for her so long. But we never gave up hope. We always knew she'd come back."

Sully replied, and it came out a whisper. "I tried to hold on to Dice, but I couldn't do it." His eyes welled up. "I didn't know it was a trade. He was there. The Blue Man. I couldn't stop him from taking her."

Her dad's eyebrows rose at the mention of the Blue Man, and he placed his body between Sully and his wife and daughter, as if to shield them from the conversation.

"I'm sure you did what you could, son," he said in a low tone.

"It might not be too late," Sully said. "If we leave now, we could get her back. If you helped."

Eurydice's pleading voice came from over her dad's shoulder. "Daddy, let's go home now."

Dice's dad put a hand on Sully's arm. "Take it from me, it's too late for that. You brought our daughter back to us. You did the right thing."

But Sully wasn't at all sure he had done the right thing. Wasn't Dice their daughter too? Not to mention Camo Boy and the exterminator still being down there. As her mom passed by, holding her in her arms, Eurydice looked at Sully and smiled. Not the happy smile of a child returned to her family, but the calculating smile of someone whose long-planned schemes are finally unfolding.

---

"Have you ever wondered where shadows go at night?" Eurydice asked Sully as they sat in neighboring chairs in the Browns' formal dining room. Her mother was in the kitchen, cooking dinner for her hungry daughter. Her father was on his cell phone in the foyer, calling every relative and friend he could think of with the news.

"Shadows? They just disappear," Sully said, wincing as he dabbed at his bloodied knee with a wet handkerchief. "You have to have light for them to exist."

"That's not true," Eurydice said, kicking her legs under the chair. "Shadows don't stop existing. At night they're free to roam around."

Sully shook his head. "Shadows are the absence of sunlight. That's all. When something blocks the sunlight, it makes a shadow."

"Some shadows are the absence of sunlight," she said. "But those are the dumb ones. They don't do anything at night but hang around under beds or piles of laundry. Other shadows are different. They're the absence of the kind of light you have inside you."

At that moment Dice's mom walked in with a big plate of scrambled eggs. "I made your favorite for you, Eurydice," she said. "You know, it'd been so long since I cooked in there I'd almost forgotten where the pan was."

"Thank you, Mama," Eurydice said, her voice suddenly sing-songy. "I've been so hungry all the time I was away."

"I know you have, honey," her mother said, gazing at her daughter while she ate as if to drink in her image. "I know you have."

# CHAPTER NINETEEN

Sully pulled a paperclip from his pocket and straightened it out. He'd started carrying several in his pocket all the time. He slid its end into the keyhole on the closet door, poking around until he felt it hit something solid, then pushing hard until the lock clicked open. It was kind of fun, actually. Sort of like fixing clocks. He'd gotten pretty good at it lately.

"Hey, what are you doing down there?" someone called from above on the stairwell.

Without even looking back, Sully quickly opened the door and checked what was inside. A mop and a yellow bucket on wheels. A push broom. Some boxes of garbage bags. But the walls appeared solid enough.

The voice was right behind him this time. "I said, what

the hell do you think you're doing?"

Sully glanced over his shoulder. One of the janitors. Old guy with graying, uncombed hair. "Sorry, I'm just looking for something I lost."

"Well, it ain't in here, I can tell you that." The janitor regarded him suspiciously. "You the one been opening all these doors, ain'tcha? Utility closets all over the school. What're you gettin' up to in there?"

"I'm looking for my watch, that's all."

"Your watch? How stupid you think I am? Look kid, you want five minutes to stick your hand down your pants, you do that at home."

"Yes, sir," Sully said.

"Now get your ass back to class before I go tell the vice-principal. Or call the cops."

*The cops. Of course.*

"Your legs frozen, boy? I said get moving!"

Sully practically skipped down the hall on the way back to geometry. Why hadn't he thought of it sooner? He could call Detective Satterfield. He still had the business card somewhere, probably in the pocket of the pants he'd been wearing the day the detective had visited his house.

Hadn't the detective said he should only call if he had information about the exterminator? But this was important information too. He wouldn't explain everything. That would sound too crazy. First, he'd say only that he'd heard at school a party was taking place without adult chaperones, and that he thought some bad things might happen there. Detective Satterfield could have the police close it down before it even got started. No party, no church, no fire.

Second, he'd explain about Dice. How she was missing, and he didn't think her parents cared. But he'd noticed. The detective could check her records at school maybe, see that she hadn't showed up for days. Well, not that she was showing up often beforehand either, but never mind. He wasn't real sure how Detective Satterfield would find her, but the police had ways of doing that. Right?

When the bell rang, Sully ran home and up to his room and went through the heap of dirty clothes in his closet. He felt a bit guilty he hadn't gotten around to doing the laundry in weeks, but it was just as well now. Yes, the card was still there in his jeans. He carefully entered the number listed on the business card for the detective's office. The phone rang twice and somebody picked up.

"Hello?" said a girl's voice on the other end.

Sully was surprised. Maybe it was a secretary, although she sounded pretty young. "Hello, I'm trying to reach Detective Satterfield."

"Sully, is that you?" said the girl.

And then Sully realized. It was Eurydice.

He held the phone away from his head, not able to believe he had really heard her voice. He held his breath as he brought the receiver back to his ear. "What are you doing on the phone?" he asked, his voice faint.

"Waiting for your call, silly. You will be at the church tomorrow, won't you?"

Sully felt numb. "But what about Dice?" He felt it was a stupid mistake as soon as he'd said it. Why reveal to Eurydice what he'd been calling about?

"Don't worry about her, or your other friend either. So long as you're at the church tomorrow nothing will happen to them. Will you be there?"

"I-I guess."

"Good, I'm glad." And here Eurydice's voice switched from a sing-song tone to something lower and more malevolent. "And Sully?"

"Uh, huh?"

"Don't try to call anyone again."

There was a click and the call was over. Sully went

back up to his room and lay on his bed. It looked like the party was on no matter what he did. He flopped over and covered his head with his pillow. His memories of the past days spun through his head, circling each other again and again without ever reaching a conclusion.

Dice was gone, being held by the Blue Man in God knows what kind of underground place, and it was his fault, because he'd led her right to him at the cemetery. The Blue Man had grabbed her and grinned at him with those yellow teeth and from somewhere Eurydice had stepped out, and he'd known then it was a trick, some way to get Dice. He'd tried to save her, grabbed Dice's hand and pulled, but the Blue Man had simply flung him across the grotto into the mud and by the time he'd pushed himself up, the Blue Man and Dice were gone, and only Eurydice was left. Of course, Eurydice claimed nothing would happen to Dice if he showed up at the church, but he didn't believe her, not one bit. He had to find Dice, before the Blue Man did something to her. He had to find her, because it was all his fault. But where was she? Hot tears ran from his eyes as he rolled on his bed.

Across the room, the little oval hole in the face of the carriage clock opened with a metallic tink. Sully did not notice, nor did he spot the tiny mechanical eye that observed his every movement.

# CHAPTER TWENTY

Sully stood by the door and let his eyes adjust to the dim light. It was warm inside, and the air was thick with cigarette smoke. Colliding pool balls mixed with the beat of the rap music playing on the jukebox. Beat-up old video game consoles blinked and flashed forlornly in a corner. It took him a minute to stop shivering so he could really scan the faces around the pool tables. Older teens in leather jackets and white t-shirts stood tough with cues in their hands and cigarettes between their fingers. And there was Robo, on a stool near a table in back.

Sully felt unsure of himself, how to act around the older kids, what he would say. Didn't matter. He'd been looking for Robo all day, and now that he'd tracked him down nothing would stop him. He rolled the triskelion between his thumb and forefinger. Dice had been gone for two days, Camo Boy for a week, and now was no time to give up the search. This was a conversation that needed to happen. *Don't think about it, don't hesitate. Dice wouldn't hesitate for me.*

He strode across the scuffed wooden floors straight to Robo, whose face showed something between shock and horror at seeing the younger boy approach. "Robo, I've got to talk to you," Sully said.

Robo cast a nervous glance at his companions, smiled unevenly. But when he spoke, his voice was as cool as ever. "What can I do for you, little man?"

"Tell him where he can get some tail," somebody called from another pool table. General laughter.

"He want some digits?" someone else said. "Crystal always answer her cell."

Sully ignored them all. "She's gone," he said.

"Who?" Robo asked, leaning forward on the stool.

Sully looked in his eyes. He wasn't sure what Robo knew. Did he remember the basement in the school building? Maybe he didn't even know the Blue Man had been inside him. Sully had been afraid seeing Robo again would be a dangerous but necessary risk to find out some information, now he was afraid it would only be pointless.

"Dice," Sully said finally. "Dice is gone."

"I don't know where that girl go half the time," Robo said, sitting back up and gesturing dismissively. "She'll turn up." The others had gone back to their pool games.

"No, she won't," Sully said. "I lost her. I tried to hold on to her, but the Blue Man pulled her away. I couldn't stop him."

Robo's eyebrows raised at the mention of the Blue Man. This little white kid could do some serious damage to his credibility here, but that topic did draw his attention. "Let's go outside a minute, huh?"

Out on the pier, the last glow of the early-setting sun faded from the horizon and a stiff November wind spit droplets of ocean water across the narrow walkway. Sully pulled his hood over his head and drew the drawstring tight. Robo paced to the rail, gazed down at the black expanse of water, paced back.

"Come on," he said. "We're going for a walk." At the end of the pier they trotted down the stairs and turned onto the beach road, lined with surf shops, ice cream stands, and vacation homes, all closed now for the winter. It was quieter back here than on the pier, eerily absent of traffic in the off-season.

"Now what was all this about Dice?" the teen said

while they walked.

"She's gone. I thought…. I thought you might know how to get her back."

Robo rolled his eyes. "You looked for her?"

"Everywhere," Sully said. "The old church. The train shed. I skipped school so I could look."

"Why don't you ask her parents? You know they're loaded. Her daddy could hire a PI if he want, track her down."

"Her parents don't care," Sully said. "They think she's a problem."

At an intersection they stopped. A street light illuminated a big sign directing cars to available parking. Robo pulled the zipper of his leather jacket down, reached in, and took out a can. He shook it, rattling the ball inside to mix the paint, snapped a nozzle on it.

"I can't believe you have paint with you now," Sully said.

"Always," Robo said. He held the can out to Sully.

"What, me?"

Robo nodded. Sully reluctantly took the can from him.

"We need to talk about Dice, though," Sully said.

"This first." Robo pointed to the back of the parking sign. "Right there." Three square feet of unblemished aluminum sheet, almost glowing in the yellowish glare of the sodium-vapor light. "Put your name up. Get famous."

Sully looked in every direction. No cars, no pedestrians. Nobody else crazy enough to be at the beach on a night like this. "I shouldn't. I don't even know what to write."

"Your tag. That's all. Real fast." He put a hand on Sully's shoulder, squeezed gently. "Do it."

Sully extended his arm, aimed the can, slowly lowered his finger onto the button. The paint streamed out stronger than he expected and he almost jumped back. A black splotch dripped in the middle of the sign. He looked at Robo for guidance but the teen's face was impassive.

Sully held the can up again, ready for the flow this time, and spelled out his name in cursive script across a corner of the aluminum. The letters came out bigger than he thought they'd be and he only had room for S-U-L. He held the can back out to Robo.

"You keep the cannon," Robo said. "You for real now. Sul. That's dope. Even when you dead and gone, folks still remember you. Keep taggin'."

Sully couldn't help grinning. He realized he was shaking, whether from the excitement or the cold he wasn't sure. He put the can in one of his jacket pockets. It slid right in. "Now will you help me find Dice?" he asked.

"You was there, you the one with the clues. Why you askin' me, anyway?"

"You know people." Sully waved his hand, trying to make the right words come out to convince Robo. "You know where somebody might have taken her."

Robo only shook his head.

Sully wasn't sure his next question was a good idea, but it was cold and he wanted to go home. Best to get it over with. "Do you know who the Blue Man is?"

"Blue man…." Robo seemed adrift for a moment, as if he were trying to remember something from long ago. "What you know about that?"

"I've seen him lately…around here. Do you know him?"

Robo looked around, as if checking to see if anybody else was there. "It's weird you say that, man. I been wakin' up outside sometimes. Like in people's yards and shit, or in an alley or something. Tía Rosa say I been sleepwalking. But here's the thing: it ain't me. I have these dreams where this blue man, he walks in my body. You get me?"

Sully nodded. "I think so."

"And when he walks, it's crazy where he goes. Places I never seen before. Underground places, but I can see there, even though it's dark."

"What does he do in those places?"

Robo glanced away, bit his lip.

"Robo, what does he do in those places?"

"It's just a dream, man," Robo said. A car approached across the causeway, its headlights stark in the growing darkness, the first they'd seen that evening. "I got to go now. You know about Friday, right?"

"The party at the church?"

"Yeah, you know where that's at. You should go. Bring everyone you know." He held out his fist and Sully tentatively bumped it with his own. The car passed them and turned towards the pier.

Sully tightened his hood and headed for the causeway. It was a long way back to his house, but if he walked fast, he still might get there before his dad got home.

---

"Sullahan Kildare, would you mind explainin' to me what the hell you been up to?"

He hadn't been fast enough, and his dad was waiting for him when Sully came in. From his dad's hard-edged voice, he knew the conversation would not be pleasant.

157

Sully sat in the kitchen chair, not speaking, not making eye contact.

"I talked to your vice-principal today," his dad went on. "Seems you been showin' up at school whenever you goddamn feel like it." He stood there, tapping on the kitchen counter with his knuckle. "What the hell have you been doin'?"

"I-I've been with my friends," Sully said.

"Doin' what?"

*Oh, you know, stealing paint and spraying graffiti.* "Nothing, Dad. Hanging out, that's all."

His dad sniffed the air, bent over and put his nose to Sully's shirt, breathed in deeply. "You been smokin', ain't you?"

"No, Dad!"

"Your clothes smell like smoke! Don't lie to me, boy."

"I was at the pier." That was the truth at least. For a moment, Sully considered telling everything. About Dice missing, and Eurydice, and Robo and the Blue Man and everything. But he knew his dad wouldn't believe a word.

"The pier? Doin' what?"

"They play pool there," Sully said. "It's smoky in there, but I promise it wasn't me smoking."

His dad seemed to relent a little. "All right. Playin'

pool. Huh." He shook his head and snorted. "Look, I'm glad you made yourself some friends here. But Sullahan, you ain't got to do everything they do. Some kids are headin' down the right road, and some ain't." He stopped to think for a moment. "You're grounded. Two weeks."

"Two weeks? But there's—"

His dad held a hand up. "Straight home after school. And you call me as soon you get home, so I know you're here."

"If I had my own phone, I could text you."

His dad pointed a finger at him. "Don't push your luck, Sullahan. I hope I don't need to be in touch with your vice-principal every day to make sure you show up."

Sully didn't say anything. This was the worst thing that could've happened. The party was the next day. How was he going to make it there now? He'd seen the vision with the fire. The vision had involved Robo, and Robo himself had just told him he'd be there. He knew something awful was going to happen there, and he had to try to stop it. What's more, he had the feeling it would be his best chance to find another door, to retrieve Dice and Camo Boy. Maybe even his only chance.

"So you'll call me everyday when you get home?" his dad said. "Yes, sir?"

"Yes, sir." Sully's voice was sullen but he didn't object any further. Really, he couldn't say his punishment was unfair. His dad didn't know the whole story, that's all, and there was no way to explain it to him. He trudged up the stairs and closed the door behind him.

At his desk he wracked his brain. How would he get out of the house the next day without disobeying his father? But then again, maybe he didn't need to. Leaving the house did only seem to get him in trouble lately. He traced his finger around the smooth metal edges of the carriage clock.

He had a terrible thought: the key to fixing everything was right here, if only he left well enough alone. Why meddle further? Eurydice was back with her parents, and they all seemed happy. And Tommy and everybody else would have a good time at the party without him. Why should he assume something bad would happen there? Based on a vision he'd had? That was hardly science.

And as for Dice? Well, truth was, she was probably deep underground, maybe even dead already. Same with Camo Boy. And the exterminator. Nobody really missed them, right? A misfit, a bully, and some guy he'd never even seen. For all he knew, the world might be better off without them.

It was all just like the carriage clock. Sure its parts were weird underneath, but it looked fine on the outside and mostly kept time correctly. His situation was the same way. All Sully had to do was go to school, come home, and forget about everything else. It would be all messed up inside, but smooth on the outside. It was tempting. It would be easy. It would likely even be for the best. Everything would be neat and orderly and well-functioning.

But there was one thing. Dice wouldn't give in if he were the one missing. And it wouldn't matter to her who got mad, whose feelings got hurt, or what kind of mess resulted. He had to do the same.

# CHAPTER TWENTY-ONE

The inside of the church was a lot cleaner than the last time Sully had seen it. Somebody had cleared out all the piles of rubble, wiped things down, swept the floors. The place wasn't sparkling, but it wasn't a disaster zone either. Graffiti still covered the walls, lots of tags, lots of pieces. All kinds of writers had worked in here, but Sully recognized one style in particular. The weirdly organic machines—televisions with mouths, engines covered with veins, coffee makers with hands—they screamed of Robo's work.

He'd run over at top speed as soon as school was over. If he hurried, he should be able to get home and call his dad without arousing suspicion. He wasn't sure exactly what he was going to do. See what was happening.

Disrupt the set-up for the party, somehow. Maybe Robo was around and he could convince him to call it off.

The late afternoon light shone red and purple through a stained-glass window above the entrance, its glowing colors a contrast with the grittiness of the church's interior. He gazed up at it, trying to figure out the strange scene it depicted. In the foreground, pigs ran into a river. A few had already plunged in the water, their snouts barely above the water, the current pulling them down into the depths. Up on a little hill, Jesus in his beard and robe touched an unclothed man whose body flailed, his arms and legs bent at odd angles. It reminded Sully of Robo in the school basement. Dark shapes flew from the unclothed man, demons with skeletal faces. They seemed to be entering the pigs. Were they the ones causing the pigs to drown themselves?

There was a sound behind him and Sully whirled. At first he didn't see anything, but after a moment he spotted somebody sitting in one of the pews. A little girl. Eurydice. Somehow, he wasn't really surprised to see her. *Who else would it be?* he said to himself. He walked over to where she sat, kicking her legs under the bench.

"What are you doing here?" Sully asked.

"Sitting." She smiled sweetly at him.

"Do your parents know you're here?"

"They're asleep now. They sleep when I tell them to."

Her words slid into his ears like cold worms. He decided he didn't really like conversations with Eurydice. She patted the seat next to her. Reluctantly he sat. He did have a lot of questions for her. Information he'd need to know when he went to get Dice. Eurydice continued kicking her legs.

"So," he said, to keep the conversation going. "You must like it here. Being outside."

"I do," she said. "My mother says I'll go to school soon."

"That'll be good. You can make some friends there."

"I will," Eurydice agreed. "I don't have all my power out here. But I think they'll still do everything I say."

"That doesn't sound like a good way to make friends," Sully said.

"I'm not sure you're the best person to talk to about making friends."

Sully almost winced. The comment stung. He had to smile though, to hear her talk to him like that. "You're not really a little girl, you know," Sully said. He was reminding himself as much as her. "You're older than I am."

"I'm eighteen," Eurydice said. "My birthday was last week."

"Yes, I know," Sully said. "You were gone for thirteen years."

Eurydice stopped kicking. She got an expression on her face, and Sully knew what it was. It was the same expression Dice had when he had broken one of her rules.

Sully tried to think of something sympathetic to say to her, to keep her talking. "It must have been hard for you, down there."

She started kicking again. "At first. After Dice was born it got easier."

"Why is that?"

"Because she has my name."

Sully shook his head. "I don't understand."

Eurydice gave him a withering look. "The Hunger can only feed on you when you're in the dark with him down there. But when my sister was born and my parents gave her my same name, it connected us. My soul was only partly down there, and it was partly out here. So the Hunger couldn't hurt me anymore."

"So why didn't you leave then?" Sully asked.

"He wouldn't let me. Because he had fallen in love

with me."

"He fell in love with you," Sully repeated. He knew what the words meant, but they didn't seem to make sense in this situation.

"Yes, that's right," Eurydice said. "He'd do anything for me."

*Anything but let you leave*, he thought. *A funny way to show someone you love her.* But Sully held his thoughts inside.

Eurydice didn't seem to notice and went on. "So you'll be here tonight for the wedding." It was a statement, not a question.

"What? Where?" Now he was really confused.

"Here, like I said," she said. "In this church. Where else?"

"But," Sully said, trying to think of how to respond. "But, what about the party? I thought that was going to be here?"

"The wedding party!" Eurydice said. A car pulled up outside the church and the horn honked twice. Her voice turned hard and cold, the way it sometimes did. "And after the party the feasting. But you'll see about that." She stood up and trotted to the door.

"Where are you going?" he called.

"My ride's here," Eurydice replied without turning

around. Sully's first thought was that it must be her parents, but through the doorway he saw the vehicle was a van. A white panel van.

He ran to the front of the church but it was too late. She was already in the passenger seat and the van was pulling into the street. But on the side were the words he was afraid would be there: *Jim's Pest Control Service.*

---

Sully sat at the kitchen table, waiting for his dad to get home. It was past nine o'clock, less than an hour until the party started. Or the wedding, or whatever it was. Pizza sat cold and untouched on the kitchen table. Sully'd been rehearsing what he'd say. There had to be some way to convince his dad to let him go out for the evening.

The front door opened with a bang and closed again with a slam. His father staggered into the kitchen. From the smell it was clear he'd been drinking at a bar. It occurred to Sully that if he got a beer out from the fridge for his dad and kept 'em coming, his dad would pass out at some point and he'd be free for the evening. But he didn't want to do that. Not even tonight.

"Got to shelebrate, boy," his dad said. Sully wasn't sure when he'd ever seen him so drunk, and that was saying something. "Had a sale today."

167

"You did? That's great," Sully said.

"Old lady." He took out a beer and popped the top. "New car. She'll be all right." "Yeah," Sully agreed. "With her new car to drive around."

"Fixed income," his dad said. "But manager said go for it, Jim. So I did. She'll be all right." He focused his eyes on a jelly stain on the table. "Why ain't you wiped this table yet?" His voice had a sudden angry undercurrent.

"I'll do it now," Sully said quickly. He picked up a dishrag and ran it under the tap.

"It ain't up to me to tell a body if they can afford somethin' or not," his dad said. He drained his beer. "Bring me another one."

"Dad, are you sure you—"

"Don't start in with that tone, boy."

"Yes, sir," Sully said. He put the dishrag in the sink and got out a can, brought it over to the table. He bit his lip. "I was hoping to meet some friends tonight."

His dad eyed him darkly. "I ain't fergot about you. Yer goin' nowhere."

# CHAPTER TWENTY-TWO

Sully wiped the table, cleaned the microwave, and swept the floor while his dad drank beer after beer. All was tense silence: Sully lost in thought, his dad lost in drink.

*There's no way I can stay here tonight*, Sully thought. *Too much depends on being at the church.* He decided to sneak out. His dad was busy here, probably wouldn't even notice he was gone.

"I'm going up to my room now," he said. His dad didn't respond, just stared straight ahead. At what, Sully wasn't sure.

On his way up the stairs he reached down for his jacket and shoes, arranged neatly in their usual place on the first step. He'd put them on later. Best to pick them

169

up like it wasn't a big deal. Sweep them up with one hand and waltz upstairs. Easy. As he brought the clothes to his chest, somehow he fumbled a shoe, let it slip right from his grasp. It hit the bottom stair and bounced to the ground. Not too loud, just some rubber and cloth, the slap of a lace against the floor. But it may as well have been a passenger jet flying through the house.

"What was that?" his dad called, voice thick from drinking.

"Nothing!" Sully tucked the fallen shoe against his body, scooted up the stairs, made it halfway up.

"Hol' it." The silhouette of his father blocked the light from the kitchen. "Whadda ya need your shoes for?"

"Just putting them away. In my room."

"You never put 'em up there." His dad was unsteady but managed to focus his eyes on Sully. "You're really pushin' your luck tonight, ain't you? You think I don't know what you got in mind?"

"No, really, I was only going to put—"

"You think I'm stupid or something? Get down here!"

Sully slunk back to the bottom of the stairs.

"Where you goin' tonight that's so important, anyway?" His breath had the tangy stink of alcohol.

He might as well admit it at this point. Well, some of

it. "To see some friends. At a dance. I'm supposed to meet them." His dad didn't say anything, so Sully went on. Quiet was a good sign. Maybe his dad was softening. He decided to make a play for sympathy. "It's just that since Mom left—"

His dad's arm snapped. Sully fell backwards from the impact of the punch to his gut. He didn't even realize what had happened at first, and then, as the pain spread through his abdomen, he realized. His dad had hit him. Hard. So hard he couldn't draw air into his lungs and lay heaving and shaking on the floor, his jacket and shoes still clutched to his chest. He felt grit and dirt on the floorboards pressing into his skin, reminding him he hadn't gotten around to sweeping and mopping the floor like he'd intended.

He caught his breath, lifted his head to see. His dad's face was almost as shocked as his own must have been. And then the silver came down over his eyes and he wanted to stop it but he couldn't, a molten tide washing his regular vision away.

His dad sat in a chair at the kitchen table, the same one they still had, though not the same house. Three houses ago. Hot Springs, Arkansas, if Sully had it straight. *How long ago was that? Four years, I think.* His dad appeared younger: a few pounds lighter, less gray flecking his hair, not as much worry creasing wrinkles across his face.

Sully's mother came into the room and his heart jumped to see her again. This must have been almost the end, before she'd left. Her red hair cascaded in curls around her shoulders. He felt shame that he'd almost forgotten exactly what she looked like, the pale delicate features, the spacing of her green eyes. She had the triskelion pinned to her sweater. His excitement faded when he saw her face turn angry, her sunken cheeks flush, her mouth twist. This was not one of the good times.

She began yelling at his dad. His dad pushed the chair back and stood, yelled back. It was a typical scene, they had argued often in those last few months. Didn't matter what the argument was about, they'd tangled about everything. Money. Jobs. Which television channel to watch. Where his mom disappeared to when she didn't show up for a couple days.

This time was different though. Sully's dad approached her, patted something in her jeans pocket. She pulled it out, held it in front of him. *You mean this?* her mouth seemed to say. It was a baggie filled with white flakes like shredded coconut and a little metallic pipe. His dad grabbed it from her, tossed it on the floor where the contents spilled out. For a moment his mom looked like she would cry, and then she slapped him, hit him on the chest. His dad turned his back to her. She knelt to the floor and scooped the flakes back into the bag, her hands shaking.

When his dad turned back around, his face was grave. He said something and pointed at the front door. His mother stood and shouted, but his dad continued pointing. She spat at him, slammed the door on her way out. His dad sat at the table and put his head in his hands.

---

The silver lifted. Sully's vision cleared. His dad was kneeling beside him, his older self, back in the present. "You all right?"

Sully didn't say anything, only glared back.

"Shouldn't a done that," his dad said. "I know it. Overreaction. Didn't mean to do it that hard."

"You sent her away," Sully said with as much growl as he could put in his voice.

"Who?"

"Mom. She didn't leave like you said. You made her go. You kicked her out."

His dad's face turned ashy gray. "I had to. We couldn't

live like that anymore." He reached out, put a hand on Sully's arm. "Your mom had some problems—"

Sully slithered out of his grasp before his dad could finish. "Get your hands off me." He leaped to his feet, ran to the door, flung it open. "You made her leave! You ruined my entire life!"

He didn't even bother to put his shoes on, just ran. It was an overcast night and almost completely dark, only the wan orange illumination of street lights to guide him as he fled his home. He heard his dad call behind him from the rectangle of light at their front door. "Sullahan, wait! Come back!" But Sully didn't stop.

After a couple blocks he sat on the curb to slip on his shoes and jacket. He shivered. Cold night, and his socks had gotten wet while he was running. Didn't matter. He stood, stuffed his hands in his pockets and walked as fast as he could. He was glad now about the argument with his dad, in a way. It made what came next easier. He sure wasn't going back. Not tonight. And not ever.

Eurydice had said the only way to keep Dice and Camo Boy safe was to be at the church. The more he went over it in his head, the more certain he was. *This is my last chance, for everything. To stop the disaster. To find Dice and Camo Boy. To end whatever madness Eurydice and the Blue*

*Man intend. It all leads to one place.*

From blocks away Sully heard the rumbling bass tones of heavy dance music. The old church was practically shaking as he approached it, the acoustic energy inside ready to blow the stained glass windows out and crumble its brick walls like the trumpets of Jericho. He reached for the brass handle on the ornately carved wooden door and pulled it open, releasing a blast of noise into the night air.

# CHAPTER TWENTY-THREE

The church interior was packed with people dancing and gyrating between the pews, in the aisles, up around the stacked speaker cabinets on the raised chancel area in front, all lit by a spread of hundreds of candles. Some candles were tall, mounted in candelabras or brass or wooden candlesticks. Others were thick and sat right on the floor, hot wax dripping in pools at their bases. The candles near the speakers nearly blew out with every bass drum kick.

Sully recognized a lot of students from his school, not just ninth and tenth graders but older ones too. Cool kids, burnouts, even the band kids, the theatre kids, and the mathletes were present. The partiers and the studious alike had managed to convince or cajole their parents into letting them go out tonight, all shaking and hopping and moving together in a glorious, sweaty mass.

In the middle of it all stood Robo, manically spinning records back and forth on two turntables, his equipment trailing cords in every direction. He wore sunglasses even in the dim light and sweat dripped down his face. He appeared to be in his own world, not paying attention to a soul around him, concentrating on manipulating the music. As he moved his hands, the dancers moved their feet. As he altered the beats, slowing or speeding, adding blips or raps or scratches, the crowd changed its sway to match.

Sully observed from his post by the doorway for several minutes. It was dripping hot, but he kept his jacket on, not willing to join the crowd. Everybody seemed to be having a good time, but they also looked strange: dazed and vacant eyes, heads floppy. It became clear Robo was doing more than just providing a beat for kids to dance to. He was, in fact, using the soundwaves themselves to numb and control, hypnotizing the crowd into compliance. To test his theory, Sully tapped some nearby kids he knew from his math class on their shoulders. They didn't even turn their heads. For the moment they moved their feet to the rhythm, but Sully wondered if they would later receive different orders.

In one corner he spotted Tommy dancing with gusto, raising and lowering his arms in a frenzy. Sully pushed his way through the mass of people, carefully edging around the candles. He wondered how nobody had kicked one over yet, recalling his earlier vision in the church with a sick feeling in his stomach. He grabbed one of Tommy's arms but Tommy shook it loose and went on with his frantic movements. Sully took him by the shoulders and gave him a good hard shake. Tommy looked up at him as if waking from sleep.

"You made it, dude!" he shouted above the music. "Isn't this awesome?"

"Yeah, sure," Sully yelled back. "What are you doing?"

"What's it look like?" Tommy said. "I'm tearing the roof off the sucka!" And he fell back into his trance and resumed dancing.

Sully waved his hand in front of Tommy's face. No reaction. He shook his head and looked around. Everywhere kids were in the same state. *Why isn't it happening to me as well?* he wondered. No matter, he'd never been a good dancer anyway. He only hoped those candle tapers stayed upright.

The music went on and on, the faces weird in the

flickering candlelight. Sully's head was pounding from the volume. Just when he was about to head outside again, it came to a sudden stop. The silence was almost more powerful than the sound had been. The dancers froze when the music did. They didn't relax, or sit, or talk. Only stopped and waited. Robo's voice came through the speakers. "Everybody chill for a minute, and we'll be right back for the main event." Robo left the DJ table and went through the door up to the organ room.

Eurydice appeared on the raised dais at the front of the church, underneath the organ pipes. She wore a white dress and veil with a long train carried by two of the kids from school. She scanned the crowd and spotted Sully, the only one still moving around.

"Come stand with me," she called to him, and though his ears rang from the noise, her knife-edged voice cut through. He walked to the front of the church, aware that everybody was staring at them with fixed, glazed eyes. Eurydice gave him a smile when he approached, one that made him shudder inside.

"You didn't bring your parents to the ceremony?" Sully asked. "Surely they'd want to see you on your special night."

Eurydice actually laughed at this, and it sounded like

glass shattering in a dark alley. "You're a funny boy, Sullahan."

"But what's the point of all this?" Sully asked. "If this is a wedding, why did you bring all these people here?"

"What's a wedding without an audience?" Eurydice said.

From right behind him came a raspy voice. "And the signing of every contract needs witnesses, does it not?"

Sully spun and found himself staring right into the vile face of the Blue Man, who wore a flowing black robe with a white collar. *Where did he come from?* The Blue Man reached his hand out as if to grab him and his rancid breath filled Sully's nostrils. Sully drew back involuntarily, his muscles tensed for the attack.

But the Blue Man didn't grab him. He simply held out his hand, and Eurydice took the wrinkled, pale blue fingers in hers. "My darling one," she said. "You have arrived. Did you bring the papers?"

The Blue Man's breath rattled in his chest. "Yes, my love," he answered. "Right here." He pulled his hand back from hers and reached into an inner pocket, pulling out a yellowed envelope. He presented it to Sully. "This is for you, Sullahan."

Sully was confused. "I don't want it. Whatever it is."

"Oh, dear," the Blue Man said. "Didn't you explain it to him, my pet?"

"But Sully, you have to take it!" Eurydice said. "Those are the wedding vows!"

Sully shook his head. "What's that got to do with me?"

The Blue Man laughed. "Because you're the groom," he explained as if to a toddler. "Why do you think you're here?"

"The groom?" Sully said. "You mean the husband? The one getting married?"

"Yes, you've got the idea," the Blue Man said.

"But I thought you were in love with Eurydice?" Sully's heart was beating hard in his chest.

"Indeed," the Blue Man said. He looked at her with...not really love, Sully thought, but maybe something akin to admiration. "How could I refuse her anything she asked?"

"And what I asked for is you," Eurydice said to Sully.

As so often when dealing with Eurydice, Sully found himself bewildered beyond words. She wanted to marry him? What for? It made no sense. But if he knew one thing, it was that he wanted to have absolutely nothing to do with it. His brain stumbled toward some objection, some rationale he could present to ward this off. He said the first thing that occurred to him. "But what about a priest? Don't we need a priest or something to do this?"

The Blue Man shuddered. "Priests! Ugh. No, I will read the necessary text and you and she will join into union willingly before the assembled witnesses. That is sufficient."

"Not willingly," Sully said. "No way I'm having anything to do with this sick thing you two have planned."

"Why, I think you will," the Blue Man said, tapping his long nails together with sharp clicks. "If you ever want to see your delightful bride's younger sister again, or your other friend. You cooperate now, and I release them. Well worth a simple ceremony, I'm sure you'll agree." He held out the envelope to Sully, shaking it insistently.

Sully felt disgust in his stomach, but maybe he could just go along with things, for Dice's and Camo Boy's sakes, and figure out how to take it back later. Surely a wedding under these circumstances wouldn't really be valid. He took the envelope and opened it. Inside were two sheets of notebook paper. As he unfolded them, he heard whispering and out of the corner of his eyes he saw Shadow Children stirring in the dark corners of the sanctuary. The people in the church all stood silently and watched. In another context, they may even have been called reverent. From somewhere a cold draft blew in, dissipating the sweaty heat and flickering candles throughout the church. Sully pulled his jacket tighter around him and lifted a nearby candle to read by.

---

The Shadow Children rushed down the ancient corridors, their accumulated whispers ebbing and flowing like ocean waves. Dice peered at them from the chamber she had been living in for a week, the surprisingly large room filled with gilded furniture, flasks of colored glass, and odd mechanical devices. Something was up. She decided it was time to make her move.

She lifted one of the logs from beside the fireplace, coated its end with sticky tar from a nearby barrel, and lit it from the embers in the fireplace. The tar burned bright, lighting even the darkest corners of the chamber. She gave a final scornful glance at the room and its ridiculous opulence and ventured into the corridor.

Though she had explored a little, she had no real idea where the many tunnels and passages led. Indeed, on her wanderings she had gotten the impression a passage might lead somewhere one day, and somewhere else the next. Still, there was no mystery about where to go tonight. The shadows were all headed in one direction.

"What's happening?" she asked a Shadow Child as it coasted by her on the wall.

"The Queen is back, the Queen is back," is all it said before it flew on.

Dice hurried faster now. She had a good idea who the Queen might be, and as far as she was concerned, they were damn well going to meet.

# CHAPTER TWENTY-FOUR

The wedding ceremony was under way. The audience was attentive, the bride stunning, and the officiant smelled only a little like lingering death. The groom was suffering a case of cold feet, as grooms are wont to do. Sully held the candle in one hand and the papers in his other, reluctantly reading out the lines Eurydice had written for him in a neat, childlike hand. They had read through the first page and were beginning the second.

"I will taste as you taste, I will hunger as you hunger," Sully mumbled. Eurydice repeated the line brightly after him.

Sully stopped and raised his head. A thought had entered his mind. Something wasn't right. Well, nothing about this whole situation was right, but there was one little detail that was especially bothering him. "What about the feast?" he asked.

"The feast?" Eurydice said.

"You said this afternoon there would be a feast after the wedding. But I don't see any food here."

"The reception is in another place, young man," the Blue Man said. "You will accompany us there afterwards. Your friends can come too. Carry on with the ceremony, if you please."

"But where's the food? Is it set up already?"

"The food is not for you, silly," Eurydice said. "It's for the Hunger."

The Blue Man's eyes narrowed, as if Eurydice had given something away. But the irritation faded quickly, replaced by a faint grin that pulled his lips apart, revealing pointed, yellowed teeth.

"But where is it?" Sully demanded, his tone shriller as his suspicions rose. "Where is the food?"

The Blue Man sighed. "If you must know, it is all around us." He gestured to the motionless crowd. "Cattle on the hoof, so to speak." He laughed at his own joke, and it sounded like the cracking of dry bones.

Sully breathed in and exhaled slowly. "I thought so," he said. "I'm not reading any more." He opened his fingers and the papers fluttered to the ground.

"But what about Dice?" Eurydice said. "And Cameron? Don't you realize you're sacrificing them?"

*Cameron. Huh. So that's Camo Boy's real name.* Not that it mattered now. "I can't do it, not if all these people have to die."

"But... but they're your friends," Eurydice said. She pointed to the audience, which stared back in a blank, oblivious mass. "What do you care about these people? What have they to do with you?"

Sully shook his head. "If you don't know why that would be wrong, I can't explain it."

"There's nothing to explain," the Blue Man said. "Forget your quaint little ideas about right and wrong. I wager you have no trouble eating meat of the pig or the cow that has been slaughtered for you. These here tonight are no different."

Sully turned to the Blue Man. "Why is it teen-agers you want, anyway? If you're so hungry, why not eat old people in a nursing home or something?"

"Eat the souls of adults?" the Blue Man said, as if astonished at the very idea. "Do you eat moldy bread?"

It sounded like a rhetorical question, but the Blue Man didn't continue. "No," Sully finally said.

"And you don't drink rancid milk either, I suppose?"

187

"No."

"Nor do you dine on maggot-infested meat, or worm-chewed apples, or flour with rat feces in it?" Again the Blue Man paused.

"Of course I don't," Sully said.

"Well then, now you see why I don't eat the souls of adults." The Blue Man shuddered. "Moldy, rancid, maggoty souls, stringy and bitter with the regrets and compromises of a whole lifetime." He looked thoughtful for a moment. "Then again, you can eat a human too early, you know. I admit the unsullied soul of a newborn is terrifically tender, but too much of that sort of sweetmeat makes the stomach ache."

Sully grimaced in revulsion and horror, but the Blue Man didn't seem to notice and went right on talking.

"No, the perfect balance is right at the cusp between childhood and adulthood. Fourteen, sixteen, eighteen; it varies for each child, of course. Marrow and organs are all very good, but truly, there's nothing as succulent as a soul when it's fully engorged with the possibilities of life, of love, of passion. Aah, you've tasted nothing until you've consumed that!"

Sully'd had enough. He swiveled and trotted down the steps from the dais. He had barely reached the main floor when he was tackled from behind, the force sending him sprawling across the floor and into a grouping of candles. The candlesticks tumbled and rolled in every direction.

The Blue Man was on top of him instantly and flipped his body over, his bony arms belying an awful strength. He leaned over Sully's face, his fetid breath wet and sour in Sully's nostrils, bile-yellow saliva dripping from his teeth and collecting in the corners of his mouth.

He took the long grimy-blue nail of his index finger and drew it across Sully's face. Sully felt hot liquid well up on his cheek, and he knew it was his own blood. He felt helpless and trapped. *Just like that day in the grotto.*

"I should consume you right now, you ungrateful brat!" the Blue Man hissed.

"No, no!" Eurydice shouted. "How can we have the ceremony without him?"

The Blue Man looked over his shoulder at her. "Perhaps we should forget this and go straight to the feast. What do you think, my love?"

Sully took advantage of the Blue Man's momentary distraction and wriggled out of his grip, scrambling to his feet. He took off running, shoving immobile audience members out of his way and looking over his shoulder to see how far back his pursuer was. But the Blue Man wasn't chasing after him. Sully came to a stop.

The Blue Man only stood, his head turning from side to side to observe the several fires flaring up around him, where candles knocked over during their struggle had lit the ratty old carpeting. At first, the expression on his face was mild irritation, as if this setback to his plans could cause him to miss his dinner reservations or a flight at the airport.

But then, as flames spread fast and he realized the gravity of the situation, a panic seemed to take hold of him. Completely ignoring his alleged love and her groom, the Blue Man coiled himself and leapt higher than Sully would have thought possible, bounded over the pews like a wild deer, and threw open the door to the organ room. His pounding feet resounded through the sanctuary as he thudded up the stairs. As soon as he left, people started waking up, rubbing their eyes and looking around in confusion at the rising blaze.

# CHAPTER TWENTY-FIVE

Sully's first urge was to rush to the exit. The quickly spreading fire and smoke stoked panic in his gut and he nearly launched his body towards the door. He stopped himself at the last moment. He knew somehow that if he left the church now, he would never again have the opportunity to go underground, to find Dice. She wouldn't leave him behind, and he wasn't going to leave her behind either. He had to follow the Blue Man into that weird labyrinth to find her. And he knew just the person to help him do so.

He ran back to the dais where Eurydice still stood in her white dress, blinking at the commotion unfolding in the sanctuary. "Come on, let's go," Sully said.

"I'm not going anywhere with you." Her voice trembled with indignation at the ruin of her evening.

Sully didn't have time to indulge her feelings. He grabbed her arm and pulled her with him. She screeched and pounded at him, her free hand balled into a fist, but he was much bigger than a five-year-old and simply dragged her through the crowd of confused people. Near the organ room door he caught sight of Tommy, standing in a daze. He could be useful.

He tapped Tommy on the shoulder and the boy's lowered head rose a little, his unfocused eyes clearing.

"I'm going to get Camo Boy now," Sully said. "Are you with me?"

Tommy snapped fully awake at that. "Dude, are you serious? You're letting me go with you?"

"Just follow me," Sully said. He hauled Eurydice, still struggling, towards the organ room door and entered, Tommy behind him.

"Can you see in here?" Tommy asked as they went up the dark stairs.

"Perfectly," Sully answered. "Grab onto my shirt and I'll lead you up there."

"Who's the little girl?" Tommy asked. "You kidnappin' her or somethin'?"

"A friend of the guy who took Camo Boy. And, ow!" —Here Eurydice bit his arm— "She's not friendly."

"You want me to handle her?" Tommy said. "I ain't afraid to hit a girl, you know."

"You hear that, Eurydice?" Sully said. "I'll turn you over to him if you don't settle down." Eurydice stopped struggling.

At the top of the stairs, Sully dropped Eurydice to the ground. She responded with a high-pitched wail. He didn't care. His arm ached from carrying her and her comfort was not high on his priority list. "Keep an eye on her, will you?" he asked Tommy.

"How can I keep an eye on her if I can't see?"

"You know what I mean." He glanced around. No sign of the Blue Man, but there was a body lying prone on the floor. He leaned over and touched it, testing to see if it was alive. No movement. A sticky foam coated its clothes. *Is it Robo?* Sully moved his hand to the face and pressed a little harder.

"Oh God, it hurts." Definitely Robo's voice. Sully withdrew his hand.

"Do you smell something?" Tommy asked.

"Smoke," Sully said. "The church is on fire."

Eurydice laughed from where she sat, and her voice was in its malevolent mode, rather than the sing-song. "You are such a fool, bringing us up here. This is the place we'll die now."

Sully shuddered. She might be right, this *was* turning out like his vision. The final scene had been Robo, trapped in the flaming organ closet, with no exit. And here they all were.

"Let's go back," Sully said. He'd changed his mind about chasing after the Blue Man. Right now their lives were at stake. He stepped into the stairwell, but stopped immediately. Smoke billowed up the stairs in a thick haze, and already it was seeping into his lungs, tickling his throat. Hot here, too. Almost unbearable.

He staggered back and bumped into Tommy. "Too much smoke," he coughed out, eyes watering. "Go back in."

"Maybe you should shut the door," Tommy said. "Keep the smoke out."

"Yeah, good idea," Sully said, slamming the door.

"So where do we go now?" Tommy asked.

"I don't know. I don't see any way out. But there must be some place, or how did the Blue Man leave?" Sully felt panic creeping up inside him. *Do something. Find a way.* He went to a wall and felt along it. Nothing there.

"So you've trapped us here," Eurydice said. "Great thinking."

"You know, you could help," he replied. "You probably have a good idea what to do now. You're the one that lived down there. Maybe you know how he gets in and out."

"I never left that place," Eurydice said. "I have no idea how the Hunger left. But I know he'll be back to rescue me soon. And then you'll pay."

"Uh huh." Sully wasn't sure he believed her, about not knowing a way out. He continued to push at spots on the wall. Maybe there was a secret door. "I'm pretty sure your boyfriend's gone and not coming back. He didn't seem too concerned about your well-being when he ran like a coward."

Smoke was curling from under the door and already building up around the top of the room. "Everybody get down low," Tommy said. "That's where the smoke don't go. I saw it on TV." He dropped down, as the others were already on the floor.

Sully crawled and pressed any place that looked likely, searching for a loose board, a hollow spot, anything. He made his way over to the organ pipes but had to draw his hand back as soon as he touched them. Burning hot to the touch, which explained the rapidly rising air temperature. The copper pipes were conducting the heat from the fire in the sanctuary right into the little room.

He wondered briefly about everybody out in the church. Hopefully they'd all made it to safety. Maybe somebody had even called the fire department. But the firemen had never arrived in his vision, and he didn't expect them to now. In fact, reality was unwinding almost exactly as he had seen it. A few extra people in the room, but all the other particulars matched. If it continued to unfold this way, it meant death was not far off.

Around the smoky room Shadow Children glided. He'd hardly noticed them in the urgency of the past few minutes. But now, one Shadow Child in particular circled Sully, as if examining him. It climbed his pant leg and wound its way around his waist, over his shoulder, through his shirtsleeves. Sully attempted to brush it off, but only ended up with dew on his hands. This, of all times, was not a good moment for these irksome creatures.

The Shadow Child persisted, circling around his head. Sully waited until a moment when the creature crossed in front of him, and grabbed it with one hand. It squirmed like the one he had caught before, when he'd gone under the house with Dice. He held on tight, gazing at the

Shadow Child to see what he'd caught, and when he did, the silver flowed over his eyes.

# CHAPTER TWENTY-SIX

The organ room washed out and the silvery drops resolved into an image of a boy, a little younger than Sully himself, with wispy red hair like his own. The boy, dressed in breeches and a rough woolen tunic, walked hand in hand with an older man through a village of half-timbered houses. The older man had gentle eyes and the browned, deeply-lined face of one who had spent much time living outdoors. From a belt the man pulled a wooden flute, and put the mouth hole to his lips. Sully could not hear what he played, but it must have been a beautiful melody, for children ran from the alleys and lanes of the village, following him as he played. The red-haired boy was the first in line.

The man led his followers along a footpath leading

from the village into the woods, going miles into the trees with the parade of youths dancing and laughing behind him. He left the path at a spot where it neared a rocky outcropping. Stepping lightly, never removing the flute from his lips, he slipped between its boulders into a little grotto, an entrance to a cave rather like the one Sully and Dice had gone into. The opening was large enough to step in without stooping, yet hidden to anyone passing on the trail.

Many of the children had their eyes closed as they followed him, and even the ones with their eyes open seemed to be in a sort of daze. Down, down through a warren of lightless tunnels, always behind the piper and his tune. They could not see, though Sully could. They were led only by the flute's melody

It was a shock when the man disappeared and the flute clattered to the ground. The man with the gentle eyes was gone, and the children were alone. The boy with red hair came out of his trance with a start. He cried out when he realized he was in the dark in some cheerless place.

The other children panicked too, weeping and shrieking. From an opening came the Blue Man, skin wet with a sticky jelly, sniffing the air like a dog catching a scent. His eyes positively glowed in the darkness and he leaped into the mass of children with a gleeful expression. Some screamed, sensing that evil was among them, and others attempted to escape but could find no way out in the blackness. The Blue Man's first victim was the boy with red hair. His jaw gaped wide open, revealing long, needle-like teeth and a squirming blue tongue. Sully turned away. Fascinated though he was, he did not care to watch the Hunger feed.

---

"No." Sully breathed raggedly in the smoky room, trying to blink the silver out of his eyes. "I have to find a way out. I don't have time for this."

"But you must!" The Shadow Child was emphatic, his voice nearly rising above a whisper. "I have never told my story to anyone. You must hear it now, yes!"

---

Time passed, days and weeks, and the children grew weak and haggard while the Hunger ate and became strong. They had no sense of day or night, and slept fitfully on the rock cavern floor when weariness overtook them. When awake, they wept and shivered. But they were not as alone as they had thought at first.

There were others who preceded them, no more than shadows, who came and led them into the deepest parts of the cavern. They showed the children a spring, trickling forth from a black place in the bowels of the earth. The shadows showed them how to daub mud from the bottom of the spring into their eyes so they could see in the inky darkness, like fishes in the deepest sea who navigate in eternal twilight.

As time passed, their bodies faded and misted until they were little more than vapor. Still, the children remained, and though they no longer remembered their names, they had learned to slither or slink across the cavern walls and through the endless tunnels. The one who had once been a red-haired boy joined the other Shadow Children in playing and giggling as children do, and he never grew older, or even realized the passage of time. He spent countless years and decades travelling the miles through deep empty spaces never seen by men. On occasion he made his way to the surface, and if it was a cloudy, moonless night, he might even wander a bit before fleeing back to the pits of the earth, away from the burning sunlight. He did not slumber, but his ceaseless hours were spent in a sleep-that-is-not-sleep.

From time to time, the Hunger brought new children to them, and the Shadow Children would gather and chatter, delighted at additional playmates. They were fascinated by new arrivals, who possessed the physical bodies they lacked, and something else as well, something they vaguely remembered having once had themselves but could not quite explain. Whatever it was, by the time the Blue Man finished feeding, that something was gone, and the new ones were just like them.

So it went until the girl arrived. She was no more than five, and though the Hunger fed, he did not complete his meal. Something prevented him from sinking his fangs in her, some control he needed over her that he did not have. But he would not let her leave, and so she stayed, and they daubed the mud in her eyes and she saw.

She was like them, but she was not like them. She loved the light and since the Hunger did not let her go out into the day, she built her own flickering light in a chamber set aside for her. The Shadow Children loved her and obeyed her, for in her they recognized a bit of that thing they lacked. They brought her gifts they found in the outside world, little treasures or mementoes or bits of trash, and she took them and found uses for them. The Hunger too was awed by her, the one who possessed what he longed to consume, had consumed so often before, but that in her was beyond his reach. At first this created incredible frustration in him, but he grew to appreciate this balance of desire without fulfillment. The feeling could not really be described as love, but it made him dizzy and obsessed, so he took it for love.

The girl waited and learned and planned, and eventually devised a way she could be free. She waited until the perfect time to put her plan in motion, gazing in the glasses and mirrors she had somehow magicked to view the outside world. Finally came the moment she had long anticipated, when she saw a red-haired boy in the cafeteria at his new school, searching for a place to sit.

---

Sully dropped the Shadow Child and the silver drained from his eyes. His heart was beating faster than the beat in Robo's music, for he had never expected to see his own face in a vision. The silver lifted from his eyes and he was again conscious of his actual surroundings, in the organ room, rapidly filling with smoke and heat.

"You all right, man?" Tommy called out in the dark. "I haven't heard from you in a while. What should we do here, Sully?"

"The Shadow Child," Sully said. "Is it still here?"

"Here I am," the Shadow Child said. "See something in your vision, yes? Something to help you understand?"

# PART FIVE: SULLY

# CHAPTER TWENTY-SEVEN

The organ room was getting really hot now, and sweat fell in big drops from Sully's chin and nose. His hair was soaked and his shirt clung to his skin. The Shadow Child's story had cost them precious time as the deadly smoke continued to build. Still, it had given Sully an idea. "Shadow Child, are you still there?"

"Not far, not far." It swam back in front of Sully's eyes.

"Thank you for showing me what happened to you," Sully said. "Can you help us? There must be a way the Blue Man comes in and out of here. How does he do it?"

"Who you talkin' to over there?" Tommy called out. "Any luck?"

"Yeah, hold on a minute," Sully called back over his shoulder.

"You follow the Hunger?" the Shadow Child said. "Place no trust in him. He lies always, yes? Perhaps you wish to go a different way."

"No, it has to be this way. We need a way out of here," Sully said.

"Yes, a way out, I can show you," the Shadow Child said, now bobbing back and forth, as if it wanted Sully to follow. Sully crawled after. "Here, the stack of pipes against the wall, see? The pipe on the bottom, under it a loose panel. You open panel and enter the walls, between the pipes. You go down, down, down, like a rat to the dark, to home, to home. That's how the Hunger goes."

Sully checked under the copper pipes mounted against the wall and found the panel easily, exactly as the Shadow Child had described. He might never have found it on his own, but once he knew where to look it was obvious, a little door with a plastic knob, just wide enough for a person to fit through. Probably a maintenance entrance to fix the organ. Sully pulled it open and a blast of hot air rushed into his face, almost painfully hot. One good thing: the air was smoke-free and clean. He pushed the panel closed again.

Now back to the Robo problem. Sully clambered across the floor and shook the older teen's shoulder.

"Robo, wake up." Nothing. He shook him harder. No response. A sudden stabbing fear: was he still alive? It didn't even look like his chest was rising and falling.

Sully leaned over and whispered in his ear. "Robo, help me out here. We can't make it out if you don't." The body lay still. In frustration, Sully slapped it hard on the chest, producing a resounding thump.

"Ah!" Robo breathed in sharply, his eyes opening at once. "Jesus, that hurt." He looked around and when he couldn't see anything, closed his lids again. "Where am I?"

"In the organ room at the church," Sully said.

"Sul? That you? How'd I get here, man?"

"I think you know how," Sully said. "Listen. We've got to go. Can you move? You need to come with us."

Robo didn't say anything. He clenched his fist and let out a groan.

"What's wrong?" Sully asked.

"It hurts so much, when he climbs out of me," Robo said. "Like he's tearing me apart."

"I'm sorry," Sully said. "Can you ignore the pain?"

"That's useless," Eurydice said. "He just gave birth to a grown man through his belly button. He won't be able to move for hours."

209

"You, shut up!" Tommy said. "Sully's doing the best he can." He had figured out Eurydice's position in the darkness and punched in her direction, hard. His shot was lucky and landed on her shoulder. The blow knocked her backwards and she tripped over the long train of her dress, stumbling to the floor with a rip of the cloth.

She hissed like a cat struck with a broom. "You halfwit! You'll regret that. When the Hunger gets here, I'll have your heart on a platter. If you haven't roasted first."

"Both of you, quiet!" Sully shouted. His panic level was mounting. They didn't have much time, and nobody was cooperating. "Robo's trying to move."

Robo pushed his body over onto his side, his face straining. "I got to rest a while." He was breathing heavily. "Y'all go on without me."

"You'll burn up," Sully said.

"I can't do it. It hurts too much to move."

Sully exhaled with exasperation. *No time to argue. Hopefully Tommy's muscle can help out here.* "Okay, here's what we'll do. Eurydice you take my hand. Tommy you take hers, and grab Robo with your other one. Help Robo out as much as you can. If he can't come, drag him with you. We're not leaving anybody behind. Everyone got it?"

Sully took the lack of response as agreement. He

grabbed Eurydice's hand before she could object and saw Tommy grope until he found her other one. He reached over and removed the panel with his free hand, wiggling feet-first through the opening. He reached solid footing a couple feet down and pulled his upper body through, keeping his other hand locked with Eurydice's the whole time. The interior space was blast furnace-hot, and little more than body-width across, but it appeared to continue on for some way into the pipes.

*Should I take my coat off?* Tempting, but he didn't want to let go of Eurydice. Besides, if he had to run through flames, he would want his skin covered as much as possible.

He stepped forward to give Eurydice room to swing her feet in, and heard her gasp from the temperature. Another step forward and Tommy was in, and then slowly, agonizingly, Robo lowered himself down.

"Oh, Jesus, it's like hell in here," Robo said when he was all the way inside.

Sully's lips were chapping already and his face burned raw in the heat. Pipes lined and crisscrossed the inside of the walls and he edged between or bent under them as he proceeded, with the others following. "Duck down here," he called back, or, "Keep to the right at this spot." It was a squeeze, and when his hand accidentally brushed a protuding pipe he pulled it back with a start, a blister already forming where he had touched it.

"Shit!" he heard Tommy yell out behind him a few moments later. Sounded like he'd brushed against it too.

At the far end there was a drop-off to another level. He fell to his stomach and edged over the side, followed by the others. The lower level was just as cramped and had a low ceiling, requiring a crawl, although at least it was noticeably cooler.

"You know where you're goin', right, Sully?" Tommy called out.

"Yeah, sure," Sully said, though it wasn't true. He couldn't tell if they were inside the church, or had descended below it. The Shadow Child had disappeared at some point. But there was only one way to go anyway. At the end of this level, there was still another drop off, this time into an earthen passageway.

The passageway's grade was steep, and covered with loose dirt and pebbles. The footing was treacherous, and when Robo came over the edge from above he slipped and rolled into the others, knocking them down the slope like an out of control sled. With a loud shriek from Eurydice, they tumbled and slid into the blackness.

*Is it going it end?* Sully wondered as he rolled on and on. The coarse surface scraped his exposed skin and fragments of flying gravel struck his face. He hardly had time to notice one stinging wound before a jutting rock or careening fragment created another. *How far have we slid? Half a mile? Longer?* Finally, they reached bottom with painful thuds.

"Get off of me, you oaf," Eurydice said to Robo, who was sprawled across her. Robo only groaned and picked himself up.

The four found their footing, brushing dust from their clothes and testing the tender places on their bruised bodies. Still, the air here was truly cool, fresh against their skin and a relief after the roaring heat. A faint glow in the distance provided enough light for them to advance without handholding. As they walked and the light grew, they approached a half-closed door.

Sully stopped and held up his hands for the others to do the same.

Eurydice laughed. "Foolish Sully. I knew my love would find a way. He didn't flee. He's drawn you into his trap."

*She's right. The Blue Man could be waiting right behind that door.* Sully swallowed a big dry gulp, his mouth sticky and his throat parched. Simple dehydration from the heat and sweat? Or fear? Sully himself wasn't sure. He gathered his strength for a moment and kicked the door open.

# CHAPTER TWENTY-EIGHT

A huge circular room stretched before them, a sort of ballroom or gallery. A few flickering candles in an old-fashioned chandelier cast a sickly light that did not reach the room's far corners. Portraits lined the walls, white-haired gentlemen posing with hunting dogs or sallow-cheeked ladies, their grim expressions forever captured in oil. The chill air smelled of must and mold. Sully, only a few minutes before wondering if he should remove his coat, now pulled it tightly around his body.

Debris covered the floor, scattered yellow and brown pieces rising in places to heaps. Sully realized he'd been here before, when he'd followed the Blue Man from underneath the school. *Does every basement in town lead to this place?* He took a few steps, the rubble on the floor crunching under his feet. He bent down and picked a piece up, squinting in the dim light. "What is this?"

Eurydice giggled.

Tommy grabbed her arm and squeezed. "What's so funny?" he demanded.

Eurydice wriggled around but couldn't break his grip. "Let go of me!"

"Let her go, Tommy," Sully called. His voice sounded huge in the thick stillness, echoing from the far walls and high ceiling. He was a little surprised himself at the firm sense of command in its tone. Instantly Tommy obeyed.

Eurydice rubbed her bicep where Tommy's fingers had pressed into her skin. "If you must know, it's your future," she said. "Look all around. You'll be well-acquainted with this place soon."

"You didn't answer his question," Tommy said through clenched teeth. "What are they?"

"They're bones," Robo said softly.

Everyone turned quiet as the enormity of the scene sank in. The entire giant room was full of them. The heaps were really piles of skulls and whole skeletons. The thin layer covering the floor between the heaps was composed of the smaller bits: finger bones, ribs, spines, femurs, clavicles.

*Why aren't the bones white?* Sully wondered. Or maybe

that was only in the desert. The moist air could probably explain the darker colors. Now that he was looking closely, he saw some of the bones even had greenish molds or slimes growing on them. *How many bodies would it take to account for this? Hundreds? Thousands?* Sully dropped the bone he held and it clattered on the ground. What had the Shadow Children said when they'd taunted him in his room? Something about him and his friends in a dark place, deep and forgotten, while the Hunger gnawed away on their flesh. *This certainly seems like the place.*

Eurydice started singing, breaking the silence like a hammer blow in a graveyard. Sully jerked his head up to glare at her. The melody dipped and rose with the sing-song repetitions of a children's song, but the language sounded ancient, syllables and rhythms from a time out of mind. After a verse, she began to skip around the room, scattering fibulas and jawbones as she went.

Her song grated on his ears, and Sully's forbearance was at low ebb. He wanted to scream at her. *Shut up! Knock it off! What the hell do you think you're doing?* Somebody gripped him on the arm and he whirled around. It was only Tommy.

"Sully, look over there." Tommy pointed urgently.

Against a wall, under a dusty painting of a man on a

black horse, a figure slept soundly. Not bones, but a live body, its chest visibly rising and falling. What's more, the snoozing figure wore camouflage clothes and black army boots.

The two ran to his side and kneeled down. "Camo Boy, wake up," Tommy said, his tone excited. He shook his friend. Camo Boy stirred, but his eyes did not open. "Wake up, wake up." He shook him harder, slapped him lightly on the face.

"Forget it," Sully said. "We'll wake him up after checking things out." This discovery had given Sully hope for more. He rose and scanned the place intently.

"What're you lookin' for?" Tommy asked.

"Let's fan out," he said, loud enough for Robo to hear as well. "There may be others still alive here." He didn't mention Dice. Saying her name out loud might jinx their chances somehow. But he felt sure she was here somewhere.

Eurydice continued her skipping and singing while the others searched. After a few minutes, Robo called out from near the center of the room. "What about this dude over here?"

Sully sprinted across the room, feeling ribs and phalanges crunch under his feet. He knew it was disrespectful to the dead bodies, but he was too impatient to see the discovery to slow down. Robo stood next to another intact body, this one adult-sized, sprawled across the floor in a mass of skulls. Sully eagerly leaned over to inspect it. It was an older man in a light gray work shirt and dark gray pants. The pocket of the shirt bore a logo: *Jim's Pest Control Service.*

"Well, this explains a lot," Sully said. He wasn't sure whether he was disappointed it wasn't who he was really looking for, or relieved.

"You know this hombre?" Robo asked.

"An exterminator who disappeared from my house," Sully said. "The police came by and everything."

"You had cops at your house?" Robo said. "You didn't tell 'em, did you? You know, about our activities?"

*You're worried about getting in trouble with the police at a time like this?* Sully thought. But before he could figure out how to respond, a door creaked open. The three boys turned from where they stood, and even Eurydice's song came to an end.

Footsteps echoed as a hooded figure approached them. It held a torch in one hand, the smoky flame blocking the view of its face. Robo leaned over and whispered to Sully, "Whatever goes down now, Sul, I got your back."

"Thanks," Sully whispered. But he wasn't sure how the injured teen-ager could help against a hunger that could reduce a ballroom full of once-living people to no more than bones.

# CHAPTER TWENTY-NINE

The figure lowered its torch and threw back its hood. "It's about time y'all got down here," Dice said.

Sully's mouth fell open, relief and amazement mixing in his brain. On a whim, he rushed forward and hugged her, folding his arms around her skinny frame. "Hey!" she protested, but didn't resist. She didn't let the embrace linger either, though. "All right, that's enough." She pushed him away and brushed herself off.

Robo stepped forward and exchanged fist bumps. "Girl, I can't remember when I've been so glad to see someone."

"Okay, y'all are gettin' way too weepy," she said. "Let's concentrate on getting the hell out of here."

"But how did you know we would be here?" Sully asked.

"I followed all the shadow things in here, and saw them go up that tunnel." She pointed down the dark passageway they had come from. "I figured something big was taking place, and I had a feeling it involved y'all."

"So you waited for us then," Sully said.

"Right down here. Well, not right here, since this room is pretty much the creepiest place on earth. But I walked around 'til I heard voices."

"Why didn't you scoot on up there with the shadows, then?" Robo said.

"I don't know. It's weird. I been trying to leave for a week but every time I think I find a way out, I can't use it. Like I just can't make my feet move or something."

"Oh, that's because of me," Eurydice said.

Dice froze and she and Eurydice locked gazes, immobile, unblinking. It was the first meeting of the two sisters, but a slight widening of their irises betrayed their instant recognition. Each mirrored the other with her slight movements: a flare of the nostrils, a twitch of a finger, a drop of sweat. Sully had the feeling if he put his hand between their gazes it would burn to a crisp. Was this a contest? A test of wills? If so, Eurydice lost with a gasp and a twist of her head, as if she'd been slapped.

"You have something of mine," she said in a small

tone. "And I need it back."

Dice sniffed and turned her back. "So where do we go now?" she said to the others.

"You go nowhere," Eurydice said from behind her. "You know you're still in his trap, right? Here in his realm, where he has all his—"

"Shut it," Dice said with a raise of her open palm and a blade's edge in her voice. Eurydice glared resentfully but remained silent. "Now, anybody have any ideas?"

"Why doesn't she tell us how to get out?" Tommy said, nodding at Eurydice.

"Why should I tell you anything?" Eurydice snapped.

"If you don't want to tell us, we can sure make you," he said, taking a step toward her.

"Never," she hissed back.

"Stop!" Sully shouted, and Tommy did. "Even if she led us somewhere, do you think we could trust her? We've got to figure it out ourselves. Anyway, first thing, we have to wake these two up." He pointed at Camo Boy and the exterminator.

"Oh, that's never going to work," Dice said. "I been working on them for days. They're sleepin' the sleep of the dead."

"Yeah, I know the feeling," Robo muttered.

"Come on, we'll carry 'em," Tommy said. "Sully and Dice can carry Camo Boy, and me and Robo can get the old guy."

Robo looked doubtfully at the exterminator, walking around him, nudging his oversized belly with his shoe. "Maybe we can try it. I don't know. He looks pretty heavy, and I ain't feelin' too good."

"You wanna get out of this crazy place or not?" Tommy said.

"Look, you try squeezing a six-foot blue demon out of your guts and see if you feel like lifting fat dudes after that."

"You ain't even tried!" Tommy said. "Maybe if you weren't so busy huffin' paint all the time you wouldn't feel sick."

"Hey!" Dice said. "You two, cut it out!"

Sully glanced around. "Where's Eurydice?"

They all looked now. She was gone. A door on the far side of the room slammed closed.

# CHAPTER THIRTY

"She went that way!" Tommy yelled, already crossing the room at a run that sent bones spinning in the air with each step. "Get her!"

He was at the door and yanked it open in an instant, the others close behind him. The wan light from Dice's torch provided a brief glimpse of Eurydice in a stone hallway beyond, just as she turned a corner and they lost sight of her. They chased her down corridors and through doors, descending a spiral staircase and cutting through a room filled with suits of armor, around a narrow snaking passage they had to squeeze through, and on and on through an endless succession of rooms and spaces. Panting and sweating, they almost grabbed her a few times but somehow Eurydice always kept a step ahead of them, using her knowledge of the place to duck through hidden openings or around pillars whenever they nearly had her. Her escapes were so convenient it seemed almost as if she were actually creating doors when she needed them.

Finally they passed into some sort of industrial utility area filled with huge boilers, the sounds of their steps echoing off the metal walls. In the center of the room Eurydice climbed a metal ladder up a shaft. The others were just in time to see her slip out a round hatch at the top.

"She's up there!" Tommy yelled. "We can still catch her!"

Hand over hand, he practically flew up the ladder, Robo and Sully behind. But when Dice reached out to take the first rung, she couldn't put her hand around it.

Sully sensed she wasn't following. "What's wrong?" he called back.

"I can't do it," she said.

"Put down the torch," Sully said, holding on with one hand and gesturing for her to come up with the other. "Use both hands."

"It's not that!" Dice said vehemently. "I can't even put my hand on the ladder." She pushed her hand toward it, but it repelled her as if she were magnetically charged.

"This happened before. Whenever I find a way out, I can't make myself go."

"I'll come back down and help you," Sully said, already descending.

"No, stop," Dice said. "It won't make any difference. It's *her*. You go up and catch her."

"I'm not leaving you," Sully said.

"It won't do any good. Go fix things. Those two dumbasses you're with can't do it on their own."

*Go fix things*, Sully thought. *I can do that. Like a clock.* Out loud, he said, "I'll be back for you as soon as I can."

"I know," Dice said. "You did it once already."

Sully climbed to the top of the ladder and through the opening. Up top, he knew instantly where he was. The light of a full moon reflected off the corrugated metal roof of the train shed.

Tommy already had Eurydice pinned on the roof, his knees forcing her shoulders down, while Robo stood glowering over them. The wind was biting cold. A pair of headlights crossed the bridge, the whoosh of car tires on the highway deck loud in the night.

Sully strode across the roof. He felt fury rising in him. It was all he could do to keep himself from kicking the little girl in the face. "You had to pick the train shed, didn't you!" he hissed at Eurydice.

Tommy kept her prone, but when she twisted her head up to look at Sully she had a wicked grin on her face. "The perfect place, don't you think?"

"What's so great about this place?" Tommy asked.

"Don't worry about it," Sully said.

Eurydice laughed. "It's Dice's special place. The one she shared with only one other person in the world: Sullahan. How glorious that we all end up here now!"

At that moment, the Blue Man stepped out from behind the industrial tank. He still wore the black robe from earlier in the evening. Sully had no idea how he'd gotten here. Or maybe he'd been waiting here the whole time, some sort of prearranged scheme with Eurydice.

The Blue Man nodded his head in Tommy's direction but spoke to Sully. "I'll thank you to have your minion release the bride."

Sully signaled to Tommy, who let go and rose with a disapproving clicking sound. "He's not my minion, you know," Sully said.

"Of course not." The Blue Man bared his yellow teeth. Sully wasn't sure if the expression was a snarl or a grin.

Eurydice took her place at the Blue Man's side, her formerly crisp white wedding dress shredded and filthy.

Still, her face was triumphant now that she stood next to her protector. "So, did you think you were rid of him? I told you he'd be back."

# CHAPTER THIRTY-ONE

On the metal rooftop, drizzle began to fall. Tiny droplets spotted Sully's glasses, not enough to bother wiping but giving the scene an unearthly sheen. He stood before Eurydice and the Blue Man, and realized he was exhausted from the long night. His muscles ached, his head throbbed and fuzzed, his skin itched and flaked from exposure to the alternating heat and cold. He longed to lie down in a bed and go to sleep, but he couldn't do that until this was all over. Maybe he should just give in. Eurydice and the Blue Man would win anyway. Why fight it? *But Dice would fight it, and she's waiting down below.* He straightened his back, raised his head. He would stay strong for her.

Closing his thin blue lips over his teeth, the Blue Man raised one crooked finger and pointed at Tommy and

Robo in turn. "One. Two. Perfect. Two witnesses are sufficient for our purpose, no? Let us continue where we left off earlier."

Robo stepped in front of Sully. "Whatever you want from him, you go through me first."

The Blue Man cocked his head to peer at this new annoyance and his eyes widened with recognition. "Ah, Roberto, a true surprise to see you..." He faltered, as if searching for the right way to finish the sentence.

"Among the living?" Robo said.

"I was going to say, face to face." The Blue Man had seemed off-balance for a moment, but now he had found his composure. "Finally, to meet like this, after our previous intimate acquaintance."

Robo's eyes squinted. "Intimately acquainted? *Viejo*, you know nothing about me."

"On the contrary, I know everything about you." The Blue Man smiled and it was like ice cracking on his face. "I have seen through your eyes, walked in your shoes, in the most literal sense. And you served me well."

Robo gritted his teeth. "I didn't serve you at all. I fought you every single second you were in me."

"A valiant effort I'm sure. But brave as you were, I know how weak you really are. How you wake up in the middle of the night, clammy and shaking. How your tough exterior is only a shell, while inside you're eaten up by your secret fear."

"Robo ain't scared of nothin'," Tommy blurted out.

The Blue Man laughed and Eurydice joined in, a pair of hyenas yelping. The Blue Man spoke a single word: "Javier."

Robo's fists tightened and he glared at the Blue Man.

"Who's Javier?" Tommy asked.

"Oh, hasn't he told you?" the Blue Man asked, still grinning. "Let me fill you in."

At that, Robo charged the Blue Man, his head down, fists flying. The Blue Man shunted him aside as easily as he might have tossed a handbag, and Robo went sprawling on the slick metal surface. He tried to stand but the Blue Man made a signal of some sort with his hand and Robo fell down with a cry of pain.

"What did you do to him?" Sully demanded. "Let him go!"

"Very well," the Blue Man said. "I will do it for you, Sullahan, since you are the groom and it is your special night. So long as Roberto does not forget I still have control over him." He made another hand motion and Robo's body relaxed, as if released from a heavy weight.

Robo pushed himself up, his expression sullen. "Not as much control as you think," Robo said. "Things are different now."

The Blue Man turned back to Sully brusquely. "Never mind him. Of what were we speaking? Before the interruption?" Nobody answered but the Blue Man went on anyway. "Ah yes, Javier Lopez. Roberto's late, unlamented brother."

"If Robo doesn't want you to talk about it, then I don't want to hear it," Sully said.

"Oh, don't be a spoilsport, Sullahan. It is such an entertaining story, and not too long in the telling." He cleared his throat as if speaking at a podium before a paying audience. "You see, Roberto looked up to his brother Javier as a Roman to his emperor. But Javier died, three years ago. A bullet in his chest, victim of a neighborhood dispute. Another poor youth killed, mourned for a short while and forgotten. Not long after, dear Tia Rosa moved the whole family to this charming town, a haven from the dangers of the big city."

He outstretched a withered blue finger and brushed it against Robo's face. Robo shoved it away. "Just say what you got to say and get it over with."

"So touchy," the Blue Man said. "But understandably

so. You see, deep in Roberto's heart, it is his great dread that he will share the fate of his brother: dead before adulthood, completely unremembered. Have you ever wondered why he is so single-mindedly dedicated to defacing every alley and street sign he comes across? It is because he is determined not to suffer his brother's fate. Even if he dies, his name will live on, spray painted so copiously across every blank surface in Moorestown."

Robo stuck out his chest and glared at the Blue Man.

The Blue Man smiled, and when he spoke his voice was larded with condescension. "I do have good news for you, though, Roberto. No matter whether you turn up living or dead in the morning, I assure you, your wish will come true. Your name will certainly not be forgotten. On the contrary—you are on the brink of making history, to be remembered for centuries!"

"Whatever," Robo said.

"Don't believe me? Look, over there." The Blue Man gestured beyond the roof to where the lights of Moorestown's warehouse district spread before them, and past that to the city's compact downtown. In the distance, red and white lights glimmered. "Do you know what place that is?"

Sully squinted. Spitting rain and patches of mist cut

the visibility, but even from here the lights were obviously fire trucks. He knew instantly which building must be on fire. "It's the church."

"You are correct," the Blue Man said. "Burned to ashes, and filled with children. They were to have been my great banquet, but dying in a fire suits my purposes nearly as well, if not my belly. What a tragedy, Roberto! How could you have done such a thing?"

"What's all that got to do with me?" Robo said through clenched teeth.

"Everything, my dear boy. Do you not see?"

Robo shook his head, so the Blue Man went on.

"When the reporters and parents look into it, when the inquiry reports, whose name will be on their lips? Who was responsible? Who is to blame? Who will they say it was who lured hundreds of schoolchildren to an abandoned, unsafe house of worship, lacking exits or proper ventilation, crammed with electrical amplification equipment?"

"That wasn't me!" Robo said. "That was you inside me, forcing me to do it!"

"Why, I don't think the newspapers will draw such a fine distinction." The Blue Man tapped the nails of his fingers together with a clattering sound. "They will say it was the result of a fallen candle, or a frayed wire, perhaps even arson. All with a terrible consequence for the multitude gathered at an illegal dance party. And they will find out the culprit was you, Roberto. You conceived the idea. You spread the flyers. You set up the event. Most importantly, you neglected the safety measures. It was you who brought about the deaths of nearly every boy and girl in this town between the ages of twelve and seventeen. Magnificent, sir! Your name shall resound through the ages!"

The enormity of what was happening—had already happened—in the church struck Sully in his stomach, right in the spot where his father had punched him earlier in the evening. He'd somehow hoped, or assumed, that all the kids in the church had made it out alive. But the Blue Man was right. How could they have, when he himself had only been able to lead his friends to safety because of the Shadow Child who'd helped them?

All those kids gone, everybody he knew from school, trapped in the building and burned to death. They'd never been friendly to him, but they'd certainly never done anything to deserve that. And to blame it on Robo, who hadn't even been in control of his own body. His stomach churned, bile stirring and climbing up his throat.

He swallowed and pushed it back down.

"Why?" he asked the Blue Man. The word came out choked but he forced himself on. "Why would you do all this? To Robo? What do you have against him?"

"I have nothing against Roberto," the Blue Man said. "Don't you see, Sullahan? Haven't you yet grasped it?"

# CHAPTER THIRTY-TWO

"No, I don't understand," Sully said, shaking his head. A stinging cold salt wind blew up from the ocean and across the rooftop. Sully pulled his jacket tight and put his hands in his pockets. Something metallic and cold was in there: the can of spray paint Robo had given him at the pier. Sully fingered it nervously while he spoke. "I don't get any of it. Why involve Robo at all?"

"Roberto is only a tool." The Blue Man enunciated each word distinctly, as if Sully were too slow to grasp them. "I crave the children. I smell their blood from miles away. Even standing here my mouth tingles with the aroma of you and your friends. But my visage is terrible and children will not follow me."

Eurydice put her hand on his arm. "I followed you, my

love."

The Blue Man gave her an indulgent smile. "Ah, but you were hardly a normal child, my dear. That is the heart of my quandary. What I need most in this world I cannot acquire but by deception."

The story the Shadow Child had showed him in the organ room popped into Sully's memory now. *Wait a minute.* Pieces of a puzzle snapped together in his brain. *The children in the story followed a man playing a flute. A piper.* He gasped with recognition. "The Pied Piper," he said. "That's you, isn't it?"

"The Pied Piper? That toodling fool? Not I."

"But you used him, didn't you?" Sully said. "That's it. He was a real person, and you were inside him and worked him like a puppet, just like Robo."

"Oh, ho!" The Blue Man's voice rang with genuine triumph. "You are not the dunce of the classroom after all! Indeed, the Piper was a spineless one, a fame-seeker, not unlike our own Roberto. That longing for renown, that need to be remembered, such a human weakness. It makes you so easy to manipulate in the beginning, before you realize what you're in for."

Robo turned his head away, his face stricken. Headlights from the bridge illuminated him and faded away.

"I see," Sully said. *Too bad for Robo, having to hear all this. But it's important to keep the Blue Man talking. Maybe if I stall him long enough help will arrive.* "So you take advantage of that weakness to get to the children."

"A biddable dupe is necessary, yes. But more than that, my puppet must have a special quality: he must be the type of person a child admires. A kindly wandering piper, a shepherd boy leading a great crusade, an aged monk who can cure the bleeding disease. A figure promising excitement and adventure. Perhaps even"—he gestured at Robo—"a teen-aged graffiti artist. Yes, such a one can gather them in, hundreds or thousands at a time, and draw them to me. And best of all, when I am done, it is they who are remembered, exactly as they wished it. Their stories are repeated, generation to generation, their crimes so awful they come down only as legends. And I? I remain unknown, exactly as I like it, emerging at my leisure to feed again."

"You must have lived centuries," Sully said.

"Ages and ages. Young man, I gnawed Virginia Dare down to her bones and relished the heart of Anastasia Romanoff." The Blue Man smiled at Sully. "But I did not live so long to be deceived by a mere youth, stalled with your flattery and interrogation. You are cleverer than you seem, but now we've waited long enough." He pulled out a sheet of notebook paper and handed it to Sully. "Read."

"But I dropped the paper in the church," Sully said, confused. "It burned up in the fire."

Eurydice chuckled. "Sullahan, do you really think I'd only have one copy of the most important document I've ever written?"

Sully's face fell, but he swallowed and set his jaw. "No. I'm not reading."

The Blue Man glanced at Eurydice. "We tried to do it your way. Will you allow me to do it my way now, my love?"

Eurydice tugged on his sleeve, pulling his face down to hers. She whispered in his ear, eyeing Tommy as she did so. Sully recalled how she had said Tommy would regret it when he had punched her in the organ room. Now seemed to be the moment for her revenge.

With one smooth movement, the Blue Man stepped forward and grabbed Tommy by the front of his shirt, lifting him into the air. With another step, he was at the edge of the roof, Tommy's legs kicking under him. Eurydice watched with a gleeful face.

"Duuude! Put me down!"

"Will you read, or shall I drop him?" the Blue Man said to Sully.

"Read! Read!" Tommy yelled out.

"I will not." Sully thought quickly. "You need two witnesses for the ceremony to be valid. You drop him and it's over."

A slight sneer pulled at one corner of the Blue Man's mouth. "I have two spare witnesses asleep downstairs. It makes no difference to me if this one lives or dies. I will drop him and fetch another."

*Dang it!* Sully thought. *How could I have overlooked it? Camo Boy and the exterminator are still down there.* He hesitated. He hated to give in. A whimpering came from Tommy's throat as the Blue Man slowly loosened his grip and he started to slip. Eurydice giggled.

"All right! I'll do it!" Sully shouted.

"That's more like it," the Blue Man said, returning Tommy to solid ground.

Tommy sank to the roof. His face was pale and his hands shook. He spread his arms across the corrugated metal and exhaled.

———————————

The reflected light from the security lamps around the train shed provided barely enough illumination to read the handwritten vows, and the misty rain gradually softened the paper. Still, the ceremony proceeded, while Robo and Tommy watched—angry, upset, but compliant. Sully recited his lines as flatly as possible, not wanting to give the slightest indication the reading might be voluntary. As it went on, he became lost in the words, repeating his parts as if mindlessly speaking with no thought as to their real meaning could forestall the end result.

"I will taste as you taste, I will hunger as you hunger," the Blue Man said.

Sully and Eurydice repeated the words, Eurydice gazing into the Blue Man's eyes while she spoke, as if it were to him the words were really directed.

"I will treasure your warmth, and keep it close to me in the tomb-like earthen chill," the Blue Man said in his low and raspy voice, and Sully and Eurydice echoed it.

"I will give up all previous bonds and cleave unto you," the Blue Man said. Sully and Eurydice followed.

"Whosoever should have a reason to oppose the joining of these two in matrimony, let them speak now or forever hold their peace," the Blue Man said.

The Blue Man paused for several beats. Of course no one would protest, but a hope sprang up in Sully that it would stop here, that somebody would appear and call a halt to this madness. *This isn't real. This can't be happening. Somebody could still stop this right now, just by objecting. Dice, or anybody. Even Dad.* He thought about his encounter with his father earlier that evening and felt a pang of guilt at how things had turned out.

But no one appeared, and Sully's hope died when the Blue Man spoke again. "Do you, Sullahan, take this woman to be your wife?" the Blue Man asked.

Sully swallowed and made his voice like stone. "I do."

"Do you, Eurydice, take this man to be your husband?"

"Of course I do!"

"Then I now pronounce you man and wife," the Blue Man said, flourishing his hand, as if Sully should proceed.

Sully stared at him unresponsively.

"It is traditional now for you to kiss your bride," the Blue Man said. "Though, strictly speaking, the ceremony will still be valid if you decline."

Sully turned his back to them. It was over. He was married. After a moment, Robo put a hand on his shoulder. "I'm sorry, man. I don't know what we could've done."

"Nothing," Sully said. He would have thought the

244

feeling of hope dying would be emptiness, but that wasn't the case. It was more like swallowing a sandbag. A gritty heaviness closed his throat, filled his chest and stomach, weighed down his limbs.

Robo leaned over and whispered in his ear. "Don't forget the spray paint. You still got it, right? The one I gave you at the beach that night?"

"Yeah, right here," Sully said glumly, patting his pocket. *Like that matters now.*

"You ain't no toy now." Robo put a hand on his shoulder. "Remember that."

A toy? A beginner graffiti artist? Nothing could have been less important. "Sure," Sully said. "Whatever."

# CHAPTER THIRTY-THREE

Dice awaited them at the bottom of the ladder when they returned to the underground world. She still held her torch, its light now dim as its coating of tar burned thin.

On the last rung, Sully nearly fell off, exhausted physically and emotionally. He stumbled and Dice caught him in her arms. She helped him to his feet, felt the sapped energy in his heavy limbs. "You okay?" she asked.

Sully didn't respond, so Eurydice spoke for him. "Can't you feel it, sister? After all this time, our connection is severed."

Dice turned her back.

"Didn't you hear me?" Eurydice went on. "You are free to go. All you have to do is climb this ladder and you'll be on top of the train shed."

"I wasn't speaking to you," Dice said. Had her voice held more venom she would have grown fangs. She put a hand on Sully's arm and her tone turned gentle. "What's wrong? What went on up there?"

"Just go." Sully lowered his head and spoke in a choked tone. "Don't worry about me. Like she said, it's over." He pulled away from her.

The Blue Man was the last to reach the bottom, and upon stepping down he leaned his tall frame over and kissed Eurydice on the forehead. "A small delay, but all has worked out for the best, don't you think?"

She half-closed her eyes and sighed. "Now we have all eternity together."

"Let us not hesitate a moment longer!" the Blue Man said. "There is a tasty morsel waiting in the bone chamber. We can begin feeding immediately."

"No!" Sully said, raising his head. His eyes were red-rimmed but his voice firm. "I did what you wanted. You have to let Camo Boy go. And the exterminator too."

The Blue Man regarded him with contempt. "What matter your wishes now, boy? I have lost my biggest prize because of you, the price of your bride's bargain with me: my great feast in the church, now sadly overcooked. I intend yet to devour a snack this evening."

"Oh, dearest, let him have his way," Eurydice said. She gripped his bony arm tenderly. "I am enrolled in kindergarten now. Soon we shall have a ready supply of all the food you could wish."

The Blue Man considered a moment and smiled benignly at her. "Yes, true enough. Wise and magnanimous you are, my bellibone." He waved his hand at Sully. "Very well, I shall indulge your little request. Let us go awaken the sleepers."

The Blue Man led the way down the corridor and the others followed. Dice's low-burning torch flickered timidly, its light seeming to shrink from the cheerless dusk. Robo and Tommy stayed close to her and the tight circle of illumination. Sully straggled after. He was surprised and none too pleased when Eurydice fell back and tried to take his hand. He pulled it away.

"Sullahan, you don't have to be like that. We *are* married now." Her tone was hurt, but he couldn't tell if she was mocking him.

He turned his head from her and put a hand in his pocket. He fingered the smooth surface of the spray paint can. Why had Robo been so interested in making sure he still had it? Could he possibly think they were going to tag down here? Find some blank wall for a burner? Climb up to some heaven spot for a piece? *It would have to be a hell spot here.* He almost chuckled at his own joke. Almost.

They trudged on in silence, falling behind the others, until the blackness completely enveloped them. Not that Sully needed the light to see. He would rather have done without the silvery vision at this moment, and let himself sink into the crushed velvet softness, simply give into sleep in the endless underground night and never wake. His feeling of defeat was complete, and he was weary to his core.

But he wasn't done yet. He still had to see the others out safely. His story was over, but theirs weren't, and the danger was not yet past. He did not trust the Blue Man in the least, and suspected his own presence now was the only protection the others had. He forced himself awake, straightened his posture. At length, more to stay alert than because he cared about the answer, he asked a question: "The Blue Man said there was a bargain. What did he mean by that?"

Eurydice snapped her head up, lost in her own reverie. But she was glad to chit-chat. "A bargain? Oh, yes, because he helped me capture you and Dice. I had to have you both down here at once, you know, and the first time I did it the Shadow Children messed everything up."

"Yeah, I remember. They put that mud in my eyes and then I could see in the dark."

"Yes, the Vision," Eurydice said. "Like you were a regular arrival, and not my particular guest. And then you two just waltzed out of here, after I had so carefully tracked you for days."

Sully's mouth turned up in a smile for a brief second. He hadn't realized that day he'd been thwarting her plan. "So you're the one who put the door in my house that I could never find again."

"Of course. Who else?"

"But where's the bargain in that?"

"I haven't gotten to that part yet, silly. Things were complicated after you got the Vision. Even if I managed to bring the two of you here again, I would scarcely be able to keep you here. I needed someone who could work on the outside to help things along, so I woke the Hunger. He sleeps for months at a time, you know, after feedings. He gets awfully testy if you wake him up before his nap is done." She shuddered at the thought.

"What about the bargain?" Sully pressed.

Eurydice sighed. "Right. If you'd stop interrupting, I could get to it. Now after waking him, the problem was, the Hunger is really very short-sighted. Only thinks about his next meal. He's not called the Hunger for nothing, after all. It was up to me to formulate the plan. To entice his interest, I promised him all the children in this town in exchange for his aid. But how was I to get them all in one place?" She clapped her hands together gleefully. "That's when I thought of using Dice's friend Robo, and from there it all came together: the dance party, the ceremony at the church, and everything. Best of all, I always wanted to be the bride in a big church wedding! Awfully brilliant, don't you think?"

Sully let that comment go by. *How much of her story can I actually believe?* he wondered. *Her version of events seems a little too flattering to her role in it all. No reason to point that out, though.* Instead, he had one question he needed answered. "I'm still confused about how I got in this plan. Robo has the connections to the kids. And your sister had to be in it so you could switch places. But why in the world did you involve me?"

"Why Sullahan, it wasn't enough for Dice only to switch places with me. From time to time, I might need to come back down here, and then she'd be able to leave and I'd be back to square one. Plus, she's as strong-willed as I am. No, I would never be able to control her."

The others were now so far ahead that even their

footsteps were out of hearing range. Eurydice and Sully walked in their own little bubble. Under different circumstances, a quiet walk in the dark might have been cozy, but on this night it was far from that.

Eurydice continued. "You, however, had the two qualities I was looking for. From the first time you walked in the cafeteria and sat with Dice, I knew she liked you. That's one. And number two, you're so very, very docile."

"What is that supposed to mean?" Sully said. "Docile, like a pet?"

"Oh, don't feel bad about it." She liked the way he'd growled his question and patted him on the arm. He didn't even bother to shrink back this time. She laughed and it sounded like a baby bird being crushed under a boot. "You have no drive of your own. No personality. Not the least bit of spine to stand up for yourself."

Sully shook his head. "You don't know a thing about who I am." His voice was quiet but had a trace of disdain.

"Nonsense. I know all about you. I've watched you for a long time, and all you do is what others want, all the time. Following Dice's little rules. Cleaning and cooking for your father. Doing what the teachers say. You're bullied at every turn and you never react. Your whole life you've never done anything for yourself." She took his hand and squeezed it. "You see, you have the makings of the perfect husband!"

Sully reflected. He didn't even want to know how she could have seen all those things without being there. But the horrible thing was, she was right. He had always done exactly what others asked him. It wasn't because he was selfless, or enjoyed helping others so much. Not really. He had always been afraid of the consequences if he disobeyed. What people would think of him if he didn't follow directions. He had been completely afraid of breaking the rules, no matter who made them, and this fear had turned him helpless, weak, and cringing.

But the odd thing was, he didn't feel that way anymore. Not since meeting Dice, and this whole thing had started. Not after tonight, leading the others, guiding them with his decisions. And definitely not now, when he was as low as he'd ever been, without freedom or self-respect. There was almost a kind of power in that. Like he had nothing left to lose.

What was it Robo had said up on the train shed? *You ain't no toy now. Remember that.* He'd assumed Robo had meant he was no longer a graffiti novice. But what if he'd really been saying something else? A toy was also something people played with for their own amusement.

Maybe that's what Robo had been saying—he was no longer somebody to be trifled with. He'd been through too much.

"So, do I have this straight?" he asked Eurydice. "The wedding was because you needed a husband to take the place of Dice?"

"Yes, because of our souls being connected. I had to sever that connection somehow, but killing her would kill me as well. So what other way to bind your soul to another than a marriage? The connection with Dice had kept me alive in the early days, but it was also a curse, for once the Hunger loved me, he bound me to this place."

"What kind of love is that, anyway?" Sully asked. "The Blue Man doesn't love you. If you love someone, you respect her and let her go as she pleases."

Eurydice giggled at that. "Oh, Sully, you don't know anything about love. If you love a dog, do you open the gate and let him roam the neighborhood? If you love a bird, do you open its cage and let it fly away? No. If you love something, you keep it close to you and never let it out of your grasp."

Sully felt there was something wrong with this definition of love but was too tired to argue the point. "What about me? You're keeping me here, and you don't love me, do you?"

"Not yet. But now it is we who share a soul connection. We will have plenty of time to learn. In fact, eons." She gave his arm a squeeze. "I saw earlier you wear the triskelion your mother gave you. The knot with three corners. A fitting symbol, don't you think?"

*And it brought me the usual luck*, Sully thought. He was past amazement that she knew where it came from and didn't care to ask how.

"For you, I imagine it represented the family of your mother, your father, and you. But now it can be for your new family: you, the Hunger, and me. A reminder of our unending connection."

At that moment, Dice's torch went out far ahead of them. Tommy and Robo shouted out. Sully sprang ahead at the sound. The Blue Man had said they were going to wake the sleepers, but a trick like this was exactly what Sully had been expecting. He sprinted forward, visions of the Blue Man's yellow teeth sunk in the throats of his friends, but what he did see when he caught up he scarcely could have imagined.

# CHAPTER THIRTY-FOUR

"Perhaps there is a candle in one of the rooms," the Blue Man said to Tommy in an obliging tone. "We shall fetch one forthwith."

*Is it possible?* Sully wondered. The vile creature was not draining the life force from his friends. He was not taunting them or bleeding them or approaching them with a ravenous grin, pinning them to the ground with his horrible, unearthly strength. Instead, he was acting like…a gentleman. It was the last thing he would have expected. Was it genuine, or another trick?

"Nah, I got a lighter," Tommy said. "Dice, where are you?"

In the dark, Sully saw Tommy and Dice groping towards each other, the Blue Man standing between them, still in his dark robe. Sully felt physically sickened to see him standing there, so smug, putting on the charm now that the earlier unpleasant events were over. He hadn't been so confident earlier in the evening, when the church was on fire and he'd fled like a cat before a vacuum cleaner.

*The fire.* An idea stirred in Sully's thoughts. *In the church, he fled from the fire in a panic.*

Tommy groped in his pockets for the lighter. "I know it's in my jeans somewhere. It's gotta be." His voice betrayed a twinge of nervousness. He didn't like being in the dark, down here, with the Blue Man inches away. And where had Sully and that weird little girl disappeared to, anyway? Not to mention Robo?

Sully continued his silent approach, keeping his eyes on the silvery outlines of his friends while he pushed his hand into his own pocket, his heart pumping. The can of spray paint was still there. With his fingers he quietly pried off the lid, a task made more difficult by his nervous shaking. He was only a few steps away now. He positioned one finger over the spray button.

Tommy had managed to get his lighter out and was fumbling with the thumbwheel, clicking it once, twice. The Blue Man leaned over, his face just above it. Dice held the torch out patiently. Tommy clicked the lighter again but still no light. Sully took another step closer.

"Is there some problem?" the Blue Man asked. "Perhaps your instrument is out of fuel?"

Tommy replied a little too loudly. "Nope. My fingers 're just kind of stiff. 'Cause it's so cold in here."

*Keep talking*, Sully thought. *Keep his attention occupied.* He slowly withdrew his hand from his pocket, still grasping the spray paint, and positioned it at his side. Tommy flicked the lighter again. The click was extra loud in the blackness, but it did not catch.

*Just a little closer.* A final step, and Sully tightened his grip on the can and pointed the nozzle forward. But he held his hand there. The Blue Man was simply standing, not bothering anybody. There was no immediate danger. As much as he hated him, Sully couldn't attack him without provocation. He slipped the can back in his pocket. At that moment, Tommy's lighter flared into life, and he held it out for Dice to light her torch.

"Oh, there you are," Tommy said, nodding to Sully. "I was wondering where you'd gone." The last patch of tar on Dice's torch caught, producing a timid flame.

"Not much left," she said. "I hope we're almost to the bone room."

"Oh, we are, we are," the Blue Man said. "It's

practically around the corner." They continued on and stopped at a simple wooden door. "Here it is, as I promised. Shall I open it, my love?" he called back.

"By all means, do as we agreed." Eurydice's voice floated in from the darkness.

The Blue Man pulled out a key and made as if to slide it in the lock. As he did so, a gruff, growling sound rose from the back of his throat, and he lowered his body, coiling himself like a snake preparing to strike. Sully observed the odd behavior with curiosity.

And then he knew in a flash: the Blue Man and Eurydice had never planned to let them live. The whole walk had been a ruse to draw them in deep where they would have no chance of escape. The ceremony was done, their usefulness was at an end, and the Blue Man's call to Eurydice was some sort of pre-arranged signal. *I never should have trusted them!*

Sully jammed his hand into his pocket, grabbing for the spray paint can, but it caught against the pocket's opening when he tried to pull it out. He yanked and yanked, powerless to remove the entangled canister.

From his lowered position, the Blue Man launched himself sideways at Dice, knocking her to the ground and sending the sputtering torch skidding across the cold stone floor. He lunged at her throat, but she reacted faster than he had expected and she held him back with shuddering arms and fingers splayed across his face. Tommy jumped in, jerking back on the Blue Man's head but only ending up with a tuft of white, dry hair as he reeled backwards.

Finally, Sully gave a ferocious tug and ripped open the stitching of his pocket. The paint can burst free. He grabbed the torch from the ground where it had fallen with his other hand and held it aloft, pressing the button on top of the can. Paint sprayed out, igniting almost instantly with a whoosh as the stream passed through the flame.

Sully dropped the torch and thrust the can forward, his arm fully extended, arcing the flame across the Blue Man's face. The creature fell back from Dice with a pained roar. Sully stepped forward, keeping the button depressed and his foe in its range, enveloping him in an incendiary cloud. The Blue Man's hair lit, and he beat his own head with his hands to put it out. The fire cast wildly dancing shadows across the wall, and excited Shadow Children frolicked in the movements.

Eurydice dashed at Sully from out of the gloom and tried to grab his arm away, but Dice was there in an instant to snatch her sister by a sleeve of her grubby wedding dress. Eurydice wrenched herself away, only to spin right into Tommy's grasp. In a smooth movement, Tommy had her arms pinned behind her back. She hissed at them both, swiveled her head with teeth bared to bite her captor, but Tommy twisted her arms tighter and she could not reach him.

By now the flames had spread over the Blue Man's clothes and he stumbled about the corridor, flailing savagely and spitting and cursing in a guttural, ancient language. He struck blindly, smashing his fists against the wall or floor with enough force to send stone chips flying, but mostly his arms sailed harmlessly through the air.

The can ran dry and Sully tossed it aside with a clank. A vibration rumbled through the ground, almost impossible to hear above the Blue Man's bellowing, but perceptible as a shaking in the feet. As frantic as the Blue Man's movements were, they didn't seem powerful enough to affect the earth itself. Was his pain somehow causing his underground kingdom to react?

The shaking grew stronger and the Blue Man collapsed, his howls now quieting to groans. The flames no longer burned bright but continued to smolder and smoke with a dull glow. Sully didn't like to watch another's pain, but he could not turn away. Oddly, as the Blue Man burned away, his insides appeared to be hollow. Skin and clothes, but underneath no organs, no muscles, no bones. Maybe that's why the fire was burning out so fast. There was simply nothing inside him.

The tremors intensified into a powerful shuddering in the ground. From somewhere down the corridor came a distant fluttering sound. It grew closer and louder, like thousands of bats. Sully, Dice, and Tommy exchanged glances, asking each other with their eyes if they should run, but they did not have time to act. The sound surged into a rushing and then a thundering, and a flood of Shadow Children spilled around the corner, thousands and thousands flowing around them in booming waves, headed straight towards the Blue Man. Despite their numbers, they parted effortlessly around the Sully, Dice, and Tommy on the way to their quarry, grabbing the Blue Man's smoldering body and pulling it away. Though each of the countless shadows individually weighed practically nothing, collectively they had enough force to drag what was left of their former master off into the darkness.

"No!" Eurydice screamed, and tore herself free of Tommy. She ran after the Blue Man, plunging through the shadows as if wading through water, and shrieked as she clutched at the charred fringes of her paramour's black robe. The Shadow Children grabbed her too, pulling the two of them away until the screeching and roaring and the last dying flames faded into complete stillness.

# PART SIX:
# CONCLUSION

# CHAPTER THIRTY-FIVE

They emerged from the smoking ruins of the Resurrection Baptist Church, Sully first, Dice, Tommy, and Camo Boy behind, and finally, the bewildered exterminator in the rear. Flashing red lights reflected against tiny particles in the smoke, illuminating eddies and currents in the night air as if the scene were taking place underwater. When they walked, that too was ocean-measured: careful steps over the rubble of a collapsed wall, across the ash-blown restricted zone, past the police barricades, all in a slow-motion dance. A murmur rose in the assembled crowd like a bubbling tidal flow, and when the people realized it was the missing children, the sound broke into crashing waves of cheers.

And then the five stepped into clear air and it all returned to normal speed. They found themselves surrounded by EMTs inquiring after their condition, shining penlights in their eyes, asking if they remembered their names, addresses, the day of the week. In the crowd around them, firemen leaned tiredly against their trucks while adults huddled next to shell-shocked teens wrapped in blankets.

Sully's dad came out from somewhere in the throng, pushing past emergency personnel. "Is that your son, sir?" one of them asked him, blocking his way.

"You're damn right he is," he said, squeezing around the EMT. He put his hands on Sully's shoulders. "You all right, boy?"

"I'm sorry about earlier." Sully drew in a deep breath. "What I said. About Mom and everything."

"That's what you're worried about?" His dad's arms shook, and miniature pools in his eyes reflected the light. With a blink the pools spilled and tears ran down his cheeks. He pulled Sully close against his body. "It don't matter," his dad said, holding him. "I mean… I…" He stopped, caught his breath, started again. "I'm sorry too. But it don't matter at all, so long as you're safe."

Tommy's mom was there too, and Camo Boy's grandparents, and even the exterminator's wife came forward, her lined face full of relief for her husband, missing so many weeks, now turned up at this burning church of all places. Actually, from the look of the crowd, practically the entire town had come out for the most exciting thing to happen on a Friday night in ages. Photographers and reporters and cameramen appeared, snapping pictures and running video feeds, station decals on their equipment showing they came from as far as Wilmington and Raleigh. Held back by the spread arms of policemen, they pointed their cameras and shouted questions.

Dice's parents stepped forward now, in their element, impeccably dressed even at this late hour. Her mother sobbed hysterically, crying out while the mascara ran down her cheeks. She held her daughter close—not too close, but close enough for everyone to see. "It's a miracle she's alive! An absolutely real miracle!" Every once in a while she opened one eyelid slightly to check if the cameras were still pointed her way, and was not disappointed. Her dad grabbed the hand of a nearby EMT, shook it hardily, leaned over to pat him on the back and thank him.

Sully thought maybe he should feel resentful towards them for hogging the attention, but he didn't. He was grateful because it meant he and his dad and the others didn't have to face them at this time, when they most needed privacy. But he wondered about Dice, and observed her closely from where he stood with his dad. Did she object to the attention? She seemed not to at first, mugging and providing quotes just as naturally as her parents. But at a point, she extricated herself from her mother and glanced around. Her brow lowered, and she shouted, "Robo!" Her mother shushed her but she called again, louder than before. "Robo!"

Now her father came over and bent over to speak to her. Sully could overhear her increasingly frantic voice. "No, he was with us…. He's not here now…. How should I know…? I've got to find him…."

Dice's dad took a look at her face and saw she wasn't backing down. He yelled out to some nearby firemen. "My daughter says there's one still missing. Hey! Listen! My daughter says someone hasn't come out yet."

The fire chief took one look at the cameras filming this and hurried over at a run. He conferred briefly with Dice and her dad. On his signal, a team of firefighters marched back into the smoldering building. Two-way radios crackled. "One still missing. Latino male, about sixteen."

Sully couldn't tell how much time passed. He felt lost,

unable to judge seconds or minutes. Recent events replayed in his mind: the Shadow Children pulling down the Blue Man and Eurydice, their hurried rush to the bone room, shaking Camo Boy and the exterminator out of their deep slumber, making their way back up to the surface. He had been so careful, pulling everybody along in the dark, making sure all were accounted for. How could he have lost Robo? Had he been there when the Shadow Children came? He couldn't remember.

The firefighters walked out of the church ruins with a body. Immediately EMTs were on the spot, putting the body on a stretcher, but they gave up any attempt at lifesaving after only a few minutes. The body's clothes were blackened but its exposed skin was unblemished, except for some sticky foam in patches on the face and arms. After the EMTs gave up on mouth to mouth resuscitation, somebody put a sheet over it. Nobody noticed Sully slip over.

"This seems to be the kid," a fireman said to the chief. "We found him in the organ room."

"The organ room?" the fire chief responded. "You serious? That was the heart of the blaze. Why isn't he covered with burns?"

"I don't know, chief. But there's no way this kid was

part of that group that just came out. That body's cold. My guess is he's been dead for hours. Should we get the girl to ID him?"

"Huh." The chief glanced at Dice, sobbing in her dad's arms. "Not right now. The girl's hysterical. Think what she just lived through."

Nobody was looking, so Sully pulled back a corner of the sheet. The face was clearly Robo's, the eyelids closed and peaceful. *Dead for hours? So how was he with us?* But Sully knew the fireman was right. Robo had found a way to help them, even when he could no longer help himself.

# CHAPTER THIRTY-SIX

*"...and now, a bizarre news story out of North Carolina, where a historic church burned to the ground last Friday night in the small coastal community of Moorestown. Authorities believe the fire started due to a fallen candle during an unlicensed dance party that attracted many area teens. However, although flames engulfed the church in minutes, there was only one fatality.*

*"Many party-goers report being led to safety by shadows or whispered voices. One local woman had this to say after her child was found: 'It's a miracle she's alive! An absolutely real miracle!' A local exterminator who had been missing for weeks turned up among the survivors, with no memory of what had passed since his disappearance: 'First thing I remember is these kids wakin' me up and tellin' me we gotta get outta the dang place.'*

*"Moorestown police attribute the strange stories to mass hysteria, and believe a drug gang may have moved into town and used the*

*party as a way to lure new customers...."*

Sully looked up from his cereal. "C-could you turn that off, please?"

His dad reached over to the counter and hit the TV's power button. Sully watched him as he got up to tidy the kitchen before going to work. Of course, it was an easy job today. First time in a long time there weren't any beer cans to clear away. He looked like he was in good spirits. Sully wondered if things would be different now, between the two of them.

His dad leaned against the counter and gave Sully a good hard look. The morning sun shone pale and thin through the kitchen window.

"You sure you all right goin' to school today?" his dad asked. "You can stay home if you want."

Sully mulled the offer over for a minute. "That's okay," he said. "I don't m-mind going."

------

Sully had thought the events of Friday night would be the main topic of conversation at school, but hardly anybody said a word about it. In fact, the student body was oddly subdued. Students shuffled quietly on their way to classes without speaking, or whispered quietly to their friends. Sully did overhear one conversation on the topic as he walked behind two girls. Though, their discussion seemed to be hindered by a cloudiness in their minds regarding the subject.

"When'd you make it back on Friday?"

"After three. It was epic, right?"

"Yeah. Until the fire, though."

"The fire? Oh, right. Yeah, that wasn't cool. Who started that, anyway?"

"I...don't know. But the dancing was epic, yeah?"

"Yeah, definitely."

At least a few must have recalled what happened though, or at least parts of it, because a handful of kids recognized Sully and gave him strange, frightened looks, crossing to the other side of the hallway when he passed them. But their expressions turned a little embarrassed when they did it, as if they didn't know exactly why they were avoiding him, only that he stirred uncomfortable associations in them, like a black cat or the number thirteen.

At lunchtime, Sully got his tray and sat at the usual table in the cafeteria. Dice was arranging marshmallows in a perfect circle. She pulled a sandwich out of her bag and put it in the middle. "Sandwich Stonehenge!" she said brightly.

"You're in a good m-mood," he told her as he took his seat. "Wh-what've you got?"

"Salami and banana," she said.

"Of course." Sully nodded. He cut his meatloaf into chunks and ate them carefully. His appetite had returned, and his sleep the past couple nights was the best he'd had in months. Actually, it'd been a long time since he'd felt so well.

"You're stuttering again, I see." Dice popped a marshmallow in her mouth.

"Yeah, it's b-back since last F-f-f--"

"Last Friday. Got it." She mashed her sandwich and squashed banana oozed out the sides. "You know, I'm glad it's back. I've missed it."

That stunned Sully. Missed his stutter? He had never even considered it as a possibility before. It'd always been his burden. That someone could miss it, like it was no more than a funny quirk....

Two trays slid onto the table, cutting his thoughts short. Tommy and Camo Boy took their seats on either side of him.

"Hey, new boy," Camo Boy said. "You and Dice done the nasty yet?"

"Camo Boy." Tommy simply said the name, but his

tone made it clear the words were a warning.

"Right, sorry," Camo Boy said. "I mean, you doin' okay, Sully? You feelin all right, after, um, you know?"

"I'm f-fine, Cameron," Sully said. "Thanks for asking."

"Keep goin'," Tommy said without looking up.

"Yeah, all right." Camo Boy pulled a lady's watch from his pocket and held it out to Sully. "I think this is yours."

Sully took his mother's watch and simply gazed at it, examining its silver back and crystal face, its unmoving hands. No scratches or anything. Seemed to be in the same condition as when Camo Boy had taken it.

"We even now?" Camo Boy said.

"Sure," Sully said finally, putting it in his own pocket.

Tommy unpacked an entire baked potato from foil wrapping and took a bite out of it like an apple. "Hey, look over there," he said, nodding toward the cafeteria door.

They all looked. A boy stood there, short blond hair, glasses. They'd never seen him before, and from the tentative way he stood, his nervous glances around the room, his clean clothes so carefully picked out, it had to be his first day.

"A new kid," Camo Boy said. "So what?"

"So tell him he can sit here," Tommy said.

"Yeah," Camo Boy responded, realizing the possibilities. "Let's have some fun with him. You think he's lost his virginity?"

Dice put her salami and banana sandwich down. "If you say a mean word to him, I swear to God I'll break you in half." She glared at Camo Boy with the power of a thousand suns, and he shrank back from her.

"Okay," he muttered. "I won't say anything."

Dice stood up and shouted across the cafeteria. "You there." People turned from their lunches to stare. "Yeah, you with the glasses. Come sit over here."

The new kid made his way through the masses of people and took the last remaining open seat at their table, between Sully and Camo Boy. "Thanks for letting me sit here," he said. "It's my first day here."

"My n-name's Sully." Sully gestured to the other occupants at the table in turn. "And here's Cameron. You can call him C-Camo Boy. And this is Dice. And that's Tommy over there."

Tommy bit off half of a burrito he'd produced from somewhere and held out his free hand. "Glad to have you with us," he said around a mouthful of food. "What's your name, dude?"

Sully sat at his desk in his room, parts spread before him, but he didn't touch any of them. He only sat, hands folded in his lap. For some reason, he didn't have the urge to tinker anymore.

His mother's watch glittered under the lamplight, but he didn't feel the need to make it go. It was stuck where it was, and that was fine. Maybe he'd get it going again someday. And if he never did, it might be sad, but it wouldn't be the end of the world. Sometimes you could fix things, and sometimes you couldn't.

As for the carriage clock, he'd had enough of it. He didn't even want to look at the freaky thing. He took it off his desk and put it on the floor behind the wastepaper basket. He'd take it over to Dice's house and give it back to her dad sometime. Probably tomorrow.

Instead, he picked up a pencil and got out a notebook from a drawer. He turned to a clean page. He'd been thinking a few days about this. Robo's whole life had been dedicated to making a mark on the world, and the only thing he'd be remembered for now was being the lone fatality in a fire in some small town. A footnote to a footnote. It wasn't fair. All he'd had was the desire to be acknowledged by somebody, somewhere, as something special, and the Blue Man had robbed him of that. All the lives destroyed over the centuries, and Robo his final victim.

Sully thought he knew how he could change that. He considered a moment. Where had it all started? He and his dad driving into town, hauling their possessions in a trailer? No, too soon. It'd started the day he met Dice.

He put his pencil to the paper and wrote. *I entered the cafeteria, holding my tray.* Stopped, read it over. Not quite right. Using *I* and *my* made it about him, not Robo, not Dice, or the Shadow Children. He was in the story, but it wasn't his. There was nothing special about him. He crumpled up the paper and pulled out a fresh sheet, tried again. *He stood near the high school cafeteria door with a tray in both hands, scanning the room for a friendly face.*

# CHAPTER THIRTY-SEVEN

Sully lay curled under his covers, deep in slumber. It was his third night in a row of truly unworried, unbroken sleep, and he luxuriated in his rest, muscles completely relaxed, senses entirely dead to the outside world. There were long periods without dreams, and when dreams did come, they were brief and untroubled. That's undoubtedly why he didn't hear the sounds.

It happened sometime after midnight, from behind the wastepaper basket. At first it was only a light whirring, a little later a creaking, and finally metal grinding on metal. A long, silvery feeler emerged from the shadows, and another, snaking along the floor and pulling behind them a mechanical device. Had Sully been awake, he might not have recognized it at first, but after a few moments he would have noticed its gears, its shafts, its crystal face, and he would have realized it was the carriage clock, grotesquely transformed. But he was not awake.

A mop-like mass of tentacles dragged behind the clock in a squirming bunch. In its crystal face, two small apertures emitted a red glow, as if watching. In the middle of the floor it stopped for a moment, surveying the surroundings. Sully breathed regularly in his bed. After a moment it spotted him there and scuttled across the room like a crab across the ocean floor.

It suctioned its way up the bedpost. On top of the sheets, a chink in the window's blinds let through a beam of moonlight that fell directly on it. Its glass and metal body glinted coldly. The clock hesitated, perhaps distracted by the light, or maybe just gathering its energy for what it was about to do. Slowly, carefully, it drew back the sheets. Sully snorted and rolled over. One of his hands reached over and brushed against the triskelion, palmed it, and withdrew under the covers.

Perhaps afraid Sully was about to wake up, the clock leaned back on its tentacles and leapt onto him, spreading its limbs across his chest and unfurling them around his neck. Sully woke with a start and pushed himself up with his hands. He tried to cry out but as soon as his mouth opened the clock stuffed it full of tentacles like a plate of spaghetti.

Sully reached out and grasped at the mechanical center of the clock, struggling to pull it away from his body. He jammed the triskelion hard into an opening in the clock's face, feeling a gear crunch, and for a moment it relaxed its grip.

Sully scrambled out of bed, pulling the tangle of sheets and the clock down with him. He rolled across the floor but the mechanical creature groped after him, wrapping him up with dozens of squeezing, choking appendages. He clutched the clock with both hands and yanked with all his strength, unable to loosen its hold. Their scuffle knocked the chair at the desk over, and it bounced onto the floorboards with a loud thump.

The creature had completely stuffed Sully's mouth and nostrils and he found himself unable to breathe. Its grip tightened even as his weakened, and he knew he was only a few seconds from blacking out.

The door to his room slammed open and the light flipped on. His dad stood in the doorway, his face furious, poised to give somebody hell over the racket interrupting his sleep. But when he saw the situation, he ran to Sully without hesitation and seized the bizarre organic clock creature choking the life out of his son.

Despite several hard pulls he couldn't yank it off Sully, so he took aim with his fist and struck it a hard blow on the side, knocking it loose. The main mechanical apparatus ripped off and skidded across the floor. The clock extended new arms and tried to flip itself upright. Sully's dad grabbed a heavy wooden knob that had fallen off the chair after the crash. He brought it down on top of the clock with all his force, sending pieces ricocheting. What was left of the clock stopped writhing.

With a grunt he gave the mechanical carcass a final angry kick. "What in the holy hell was that thing?"

"I think it was the carriage clock," Sully croaked.

Now his dad looked at him with concern. "Are you all right?" he asked, taking the boy in his arms and pulling limp metal strands off his reddened face.

"I'm fine, Dad." Sully hugged him back. "I'm j-just happy to breathe again."

All his father responded with was, "Thank God, thank God," over and over again.

And there they sat for several minutes, simply holding each other in the now still, quiet house. After a time, his dad let him go. "Everything okay?" he asked.

"Yeah," Sully said. "I'm kind of tired."

His dad looked around at the metal and glass shards

scattered across the floor. "I reckon that thing's good and finished. Why don't you come sleep in my room? We'll clean up this mess in the morning."

"Sure." Sully said. He didn't move though. "Dad?"

"Yeah?"

"Can I tell you about what happened? In the morning, I mean. About everything that happened."

His dad nodded. "I'd like that, Sullahan. I think we're past due for a good talk."

Sully followed his dad up to the master bedroom and tucked himself under the covers while his dad flipped off the light. Not surprisingly, it took Sully a while to get back to sleep, but when he did, slumber arrived with an irresistible might, forcing his eyes closed with the power of a vise. Only the next morning at breakfast did Sully recall hearing something just before finally drifting off, something that had echoed through his dreams the rest of the night.

*Maybe it was only my imagination,* he thought to himself, but he knew that wasn't true. He'd heard it clearly just before passing out: a distant sound, muffled, as if from behind a wall or under the floorboards, but quite distinct. It was the sound of a little girl giggling.

I'd like to thank all the people who have helped me in the writing and production of this book: Pat Kallman, Anita Klein, Steve Moriarty, Barbara Osgood, and the members of the Writers of Chantilly, who have done so much to improve my writing with their comments, advice, and encouragement over the years!

I hope you enjoyed reading *Roll dem Bones!* Because Amazon reviews are one of the main drivers of book sales, please consider leaving a brief but honest review on this book's Amazon page.

Sign up for my mailing list and receive an absolutely free short story!
nicholasbruner.com/contact

**Look for**
*Mother Ink*
**The first book of an epic fantasy trilogy by Nicholas Bruner coming in Fall 2021!**

www.ingramcontent.com/pod-product-compliance
Lightning Source LLC
Chambersburg PA
CBHW022144170626
46807CB00005B/2070